"WHY DO YOU DRAW BACK FROM ME WHEN YOU PROFESS YOU WANT TO MARRY ME?"

Sally was too good an actress to let him see the battle that was warring within her. She wanted nothing more than to kiss him, but she instinctively feared that if she did, she would be lost.

"And why would you want to kiss me if you do not want to marry me?" she demanded, feigning indignation. "Are you a rakehell?"

"That is not a word that should disgrace a lady's lips."

"Why should a woman be barred from speaking the truth simply because it is unpleasant?"

Garth could not argue with her logic.

Nor could he understand how he could simultaneously be attracted and provoked by a woman.

Other Regency Romances from Avon Books

THE
FAIR IMPOSTOR

MARLENE SUSON

AVON BOOKS ◆ NEW YORK

THE FAIR IMPOSTOR is an original publication of Avon Books. This work has never before appeared in book form. This work is a novel. Any similarity to actual persons or events is purely coincidental.

AVON BOOKS
A division of
The Hearst Corporation
1350 Avenue of the Americas
New York, New York 10019

Copyright © 1992 by Marlene Suson
Published by arrangement with the author
Library of Congress Catalog Card Number: 91-92447
ISBN: 0-380-76472-5

First Avon Books Printing: August 1992

AVON TRADEMARK REG. U.S. PAT. OFF. AND IN OTHER COUNTRIES, MARCA REGISTRADA, HECHO EN U.S.A.

Printed in the U.S.A.

RA   10 9 8 7 6 5 4 3 2 1

To Katie and Randy
with love

1

&&&&&&&&&&&&&

Preston Walcott, the big, ruddy-faced manager of the Walcott Strolling Players, was vigorously cursing his troupe's wretched luck, but Peg Felton, the black-haired actress before him, took it personally.

"I did not sprain my ankle on purpose," she cried, leaning heavily on two brawny actors. "So do not swear at me, Preston Walcott!"

"I wasn't, though you might have watched where you were walking instead of stepping into that hole. I was cursing my ill luck."

"*Your* luck! 'Tis me who cannot walk," Peg said acidly.

Behind them in a quiet Kentish meadow stood a much-patched tent where in forty minutes the Walcott company was scheduled to perform William Shakespeare's tragedy, *Antony and Cleopatra*.

Peg Felton was to have played Cleopatra, and it was too late to change the play now. Young Sally Marlowe would have to go on in the injured actress's place. Walcott stomped off in search of her.

He found Sally beside a stone bridge over a stream that separated the meadow from a village called Aveton. Although she was an accredited beauty, she hardly looked the part of the dark, sultry temptress of the Nile. Not only was she too young, but a profusion of golden

1

curls tumbled about her face. Her big, beguiling eyes were as blue as bachelor's buttons, and her pale complexion was often likened to white rose petals.

Despite her youth, Sally was an excellent actress who could be counted upon to play every kind of part from Juliet to breeches' roles with skill and aplomb. Walcott knew that she would acquit herself well even in the ill-suited role of Cleopatra. Furthermore, it was her last day with his company, and he was pleased that now she would have a starring role for her final performance.

At his approach, Sally stood up. She was tiny, standing only an inch over five feet, and looked as fragile as a hothouse orchid, but Walcott knew differently. Full of vitality and ebullient good humor, she had more stamina than three-quarters of his company, and none of the difficult temperament that made actresses the bane of his existence. He would hate to lose her. She was a favorite of his and of the other members of the troupe, but her talents deserved a better showcase than a company of strolling players could provide.

Walcott said, "Peg Felton has sprained her ankle so badly she cannot walk. You will have to play Cleopatra in her stead. Can you do it?"

"Of course," Sally replied without hesitation.

She loved a challenge, on stage or off, Walcott thought as he hurried off to help the candle snuffer place the stage lights. Indeed, if he had any complaint about her, it was that her taste for adventure and her high spirits sometimes overrode her good sense, and she plunged impetuously into escapades a more mature—or less venturesome—woman would have avoided.

Sally remained by the stream for another minute, staring into its placid waters as she thought about the character she was about to portray.

At the sudden clatter of a horse's hooves on the bridge, she looked up and saw a brown gelding approaching. Its rider, a man in his late twenties, was fashionably dressed in a navy jacket and gray corduroy riding breeches.

When he saw her, he stopped his mount abruptly. "Lady Serena! You have finally forsaken your sickbed!"

Sally, flattered at being mistaken for a highborn lady, even one whose name she didn't recognize, did not immediately correct the rider's mistaken impression.

He dismounted from his gelding and came up to her. "Garth will be overjoyed that you have at last come out of your seclusion."

The coolness in the man's tone and gaze as he regarded Sally told her that he did not like the Lady Serena overmuch.

"Don't mind telling you, you are most cruel to have refused to see poor Garth for all these weeks. After all, he is your betrothed!" The stranger's eyes narrowed disapprovingly. "Don't want to upset Garth so I haven't mentioned it, but I strongly suspect that you've not been suffering from the measles at all, but from a severe case of Lord Leland Caine. Don't think the way you were carrying on with Lee in London escaped my notice."

Although Sally was curious to hear more about Serena, Lee, and poor Garth, she decided she'd had enough of this ruse and said politely, "You are mistaken. I am not Lady Serena, whoever she is."

"Don't try to gammon me, girl! Not such a nodcock that I don't know you when I see you. Don't mind telling you that you are treating your betrothed most shabbily, and he deserves better. Sir Garth Taymor is a prime cove, worth a dozen of Lord Leland."

"I tell you I am not Lady Serena."

He snorted in disbelief. "Who the devil do you *claim* to be?"

"I *am* Sally Marlowe, an actress with this company of strolling players." She gestured toward the tent in the meadow. "Who are you?"

"You know very well that I am Lord Eldwin Drake. Don't pretend to know what your game is, but you'll catch cold trying to hoax me like this. Nothing you can say will convince me that you are not Lady Serena!"

Sally smiled, unable to resist this challenge. Her

years on the stage had taught her to speak with the cultured enunciation of a lady of quality. She had, however, other accents in her repertoire, and she used one now.

"Oi tell you Oi ain't yer bloody Lady Serena," she said in a tone so deliberately shrill that it was painful even to her own ears. "Who the bloody 'ell is she?"

Lord Eldwin stared at Sally as though a viper had just crawled out of her mouth.

He twice attempted speech and failed before he managed to say weakly, "Don't mind telling you that you look enough like Lady Serena Keith, the Earl of Wycombe's sister, to be her twin. Don't talk like her though!"

Sally reverted to her normal speech. "Why does this Lady Serena refuse to see her betrothed?"

"Professes to have a severe case of measles with dire complications, but I suspect the story is poppycock. Poor Garth is frantic."

"How long has it been since he has seen her?"

"Two years."

"*Two years!*" Sally exclaimed in profound astonishment. "She claims to have had the measles for *two* years?"

"No, no," his lordship said hastily, "only for the past month since Garth returned to England. He was a diplomat stationed in Brazil before that."

"And you think that while he was gone, the Lady Serena found another interest?" Sally prompted.

"Precisely. If she don't want to marry Garth, then she should cry off. Plenty of other women would be delighted to shackle him. He's handsome, amiable, and rich as Croesus. Not at all like the rest of his dreadful family." Lord Eldwin shuddered. "His half-sister, Rowena, arrived at Tamar—that's Garth's country home—last night. Can't abide the woman, and she attaches herself to me like a leech. Had to sneak out riding this afternoon to give her the slip. She—"

He broke off, looking a little sheepish. "Beg pardon,

shouldn't be unburdening myself to a stranger like this, but Rowena makes me so angry I cannot contain myself. I shall ride on now and leave you in peace.''

As he remounted his horse, Sally heard him mutter, ''Wonder how long Garth will have to put up with Rowena?''

Garth was asking himself that same question as he reluctantly drove Rowena through the village of Aveton not long after Lord Eldwin had left Sally by the bridge.

Although Garth, who took his duties as head of his family seriously, would never dream of shirking his responsibilities to his half-sister, he wasn't particularly anxious for her company.

A spinster ten years older than Garth, Rowena was as great a social climber as their late father had been. She fawned over anyone with a title before his name. The obsequious way she toadied to her social betters disgusted her well-bred brother. Worse, she treated those she considered her inferior as though they were too far beneath her touch to notice.

Rowena had hoped to show Lord Eldwin the countryside so that she might be seen riding with a pink of the *ton*. When she discovered he had left Tamar without her, she determined to run him to ground. Rowena ferreted out of a stable boy that his lordship had asked directions to Aveton.

She insisted that Garth drive her there on the pretext that he must see the extraordinary stained-glass window that had been installed in the church. Her brother, unaware of her real motive, obligingly ordered his curricle.

He was a little bewildered when he saw the window, so amateurish it bordered on the crude, that she had praised. Surely even Rowena's taste, deficient as it was, could not be that bad.

As they left the church, dozens of residents from the town were crossing the stone bridge toward a tent on the other side of the stream from the village. Rowena, thinking that her quarry might be there, insisted that they investigate.

Garth complied with grave misgivings. Rowena loved nothing more than letting country folk know how superior she was to them. Fearing she would stage one of her scenes that so mortified him, he deliberately guided his curricle behind the tent so it would conceal them from most of the crowd.

When they learned that a troupe of strolling players was about to perform, Garth was anxious to drive on. He was used to sophisticated entertainment, and he had no desire to waste his time watching a deplorable performance by provincial actors.

Rowena, however, exclaimed loudly, "How amusing! We must watch it."

They were still sitting in the curricle, and the few people within earshot turned to look at them.

Garth muttered under his breath, "For God's sake, Rowena, the play is a tragedy, not a comedy."

"I am convinced that seeing these poor inferior country bumpkins attempting to perform a tragedy like *Antony and Cleopatra* will be hilarious. Far funnier, I am certain, than any comedy." She smirked unpleasantly. "I can scarcely wait to see what a fool the actress playing Cleopatra makes of herself."

Garth knew the real fool was considerably closer to him than the stage. So apparently did several of the spectators from the way they regarded Rowena. He was so embarrassed by his vulgar sister that his skillful tongue, which served him so well in diplomacy, failed him now. Desperate to quiet her and escape the staring crowd, he said curtly, "Then let us not waste our time watching these 'bumpkins.' "

"Oh, no, I am persuaded they will be most amusing." Rowena tittered. "No doubt Cleopatra is some aging lightskirt who can find no other employment."

In a makeshift dressing room created by hanging blankets at the back of the stage, Sally Marlowe had donned her costume, darkened her complexion, and hidden her golden curls beneath a black wig.

Unfortunately, the Walcott players' resources were too slender for their repertoire. Each performer had only one or two costumes that must serve for whatever role they might undertake, whether the setting was ancient Rome or modern England. Sally's elaborate green satin robe with an overskirt looped up *à la polonaise* and a pink stomacher trimmed with matching bows was more reminiscent of Marie Antoinette's court then Cleopatra's.

The effect was far from what Sally would have liked, but there was no help for it.

She was blackening her eyebrows with burnt ivory shavings when she heard the clatter of an equipage stopping on the other side of the canvas from her. Startled by its proximity, she turned away from the cracked mirror and peeked through a small hole in the material at a curricle only a few feet away.

Its driver had arresting eyes, brilliantly green and fringed by thick lashes. His golden-brown hair was thick and wavy, and he had a noble nose, strong jaw, and sensual mouth. Sally's breath quickened at the sight of him. Although she was usually immune to handsome faces, something about his harried expression and the way an unruly wave of hair tumbled over his forehead tugged at her heart.

Sally liked a man who dressed with care, and he was splendidly attired in the first stare of fashion. No doubt about it, he was a well-breeched swell. His starched white neckcloth was expertly tied. Both the superb fit and the *Bleu Celeste* color of his superfine tailcoat proclaimed that it could have come only from Weston's inimitable hand. Beneath that exquisite coat and pale clinging pantaloons, he was slim but well-made.

She scarcely noticed the woman with him until her loud voice began cruelly mocking the troupe's talents. Sally was outraged that anyone would judge the Walcott players so unfairly without even having seen them perform. It pleased her to observe that the critic was a fat, sour-faced woman at least a decade older than her companion, with nothing to recommend her except a very expensive black bombazine gown, overly decorated with lace and frills.

Sally detected no likeness between this ill-assorted pair and concluded that they must not be related by blood. She wondered if they could be married. If that were the case, the woman had to be a rich heiress riveted to a fortune hunter who had wed her only for her money. Nevertheless, Sally could not help but feel sorry for any man married to such an unpleasant creature, no matter how suspect his motives had been.

But when he advised his companion against wasting their time watching an inferior company of bumpkins, Sally's sympathy crumbled and turned to fiery indignation, made all the hotter by her initial attraction to him.

"Bacon-brained fribble," she fumed under her breath.

Then his companion had the effrontery to impugn both Sally's morals and her talent.

An aging lightskirt indeed! That was an intolerable slur upon both Sally and her parents, a God-fearing couple who had raised their children to a standard of propriety more readily found in a parsonage than a theater. She was not one of those actresses whose real talents and ambition lay in horizontal performances on a more intimate stage for moneyed swells. Although she had received more than one offer to embark upon such a career, she rejected each of them with disdain, and her conduct remained above reproach.

Sally was not one to accept meekly the egregious slander of a hatchet-faced shrew, and she flew out of the tent toward the offensive couple. She was famous among the Walcott company for speaking her mind with unsettling candor, and she was bent on doing so now.

When she reached them, the sinking sun was directly

behind their heads, forcing her to squint fiercely at them.

The woman had to be forty if she was a day. And she dared to call Sally aging!

Sally would have thought the woman's companion most attractive had it not been for his infuriating top-loftiness. The only discordant note in his impeccable appearance was that wayward wave of thick, golden-brown hair falling on his forehead.

. With the hauteur of a queen, Sally demanded of the woman, "Who are *you*, madam, to be calling *me* aging?"

The slow-witted culprit was so startled that she stared at Sally blankly before stammering, "I beg your pardon?"

"And well you should," Sally snapped, "for I am neither aging nor a lightskirt."

The woman, belatedly tumbling to Sally's identity, seemed to inflate with righteous indignation. "How dare you address me? Do you know who I am?"

"I daresay no one of any importance or you would be better bred than to pass damning judgment upon a performance before you have even seen it."

This brought laughter and a ripple of applause from the crowd of interested spectators gathering around them.

Two brilliant spots of red appeared on the woman's cheeks. "I will have you know I am a lady of quality."

"I should not have guessed it from your conduct," Sally retorted. "Obviously you are one of the so-called quality that display their much-vaunted breeding only for their own kind and treat everyone else as though they were beneath contempt."

More applause rang out, turning Rowena's face crimson. Garth, who had long wanted to give his sister just such a well-deserved trimming, regarded the actress approvingly. By God, she had spirit. He was suddenly eager to see her perform.

Studying her, he was surprised at what a little thing

she was. Her bearing had at first made her seem more imposing, but he belatedly realized that she was no taller than his diminutive betrothed.

She was youngish, too, not more than five and twenty. Her hair was black and her skin so dark that he wondered whether she was of gypsy blood. Thick, straight bangs covered her forehead to the arch of her black brows. Beneath them, her eyes were no more than slits, so narrow that he could not even tell their color. If it were not for her unfortunate squint, she would have been quite pretty.

Normally, he preferred a fair blonde—except when she was the selfish ninnyhammer to whom he was reluctantly betrothed—and it surprised him that he felt inexplicably drawn to this dark-complected, black-haired actress.

"Little wasp," he said appreciatively.

Apparently she failed to detect the admiration intended in this appellation, for her chin rose to a defiant angle.

For the first time, Garth took note of the oddity of her costume. His ready sense of humor was tickled by the incongruity of a Louis XVI–style gown coupled with straight black hair worn in the fashion of ancient Egypt. He could not resist telling her, "I believe, little wasp, that you have confused your centuries."

"I did not request your opinion, Your Grace," she said, frostily.

"You flatter me. I am not a duke."

"No?" she asked in feigned disbelief. "Should I have said Your Highness?"

He grinned at her, a mischievous light dancing in his green eyes. "No, although I am thought to be a prince of fellows."

It was the first time Sally had seen him smile. It embraced his entire face, even his eyes, exuding warmth. It quite took her breath away, and she felt herself softening toward him. Her weakness goaded her into retorting sharply, "Not by me, you're not."

He was still grinning. "Even though you believe me royal?" he teased. "What made you think that?"

She said sweetly, "You are so puffed up in your own consequence that I was certain you must be at least of that rank."

Instead of taking umbrage as she had expected he would, a disconcerting gleam of male interest flashed in his green eyes, and his grin widened. "Oh ho, what a nasty little sting you have, wasp. I look forward to seeing your Cleopatra."

"No!" his companion exclaimed, tugging urgently at his sleeve. "Let us leave immediately."

He replied, "It was you who insisted we stop to see the play. Now, I insist that we do so."

"Surely you do not want to waste your time watching a bumpkin like me perform," Sally told him acidly, parroting his earlier comment.

"To the contrary, I think I should enjoy it very much, little wasp."

The teasing gleam in his green eyes was having an insidious effect on her pulse rate. Perversely, this reaction heightened her anger at him. In a voice dripping with sarcasm, she said, "But Your Grace, I am so far beneath your touch."

"Yes, you are," he agreed cheerfully, "but—"

His casual agreement ignited her temper. "How insulting you are!"

"How can you say that when all I did was agree with you?" he asked, his innocent tone contradicted by the laughter in his eyes.

Little as Sally liked his condescension, even less did she like his amusement at her expense. Without another word, she turned and marched indignantly back to the tent. She longed to find some way of wiping that superior smile from his face!

"Are you running away, wasp?" he called after her. "You disappoint me. I did not think you so poor-spirited."

She ignored his provocative challenge. Stepping back

into the tent, she was determined to show him and that dreadful woman with him how badly they had misjudged her acting talent.

Sally vowed to give the performance of her life.

2

When the play ended, Garth clapped hard and long for the black-haired actress who had played Cleopatra. She had given a truly remarkable performance.

He was amazed that such a talented performer should be found in a company of strolling players, the lowest and poorest rung of the British theater. They walked from town to town, pushing their props and costumes in handcarts and performing where they could.

Garth could not remember when he had been so affected by a performance, not even one by the great Mrs. Sarah Siddons. The little wasp had captured all the nuances of Cleopatra's character. So poignant had she been as she clasped the poisonous asps to her breast and arm that many in the audience had been moved to tears. Now, as she took her curtain call, she was rewarded with waves of thunderous applause and shouts of bravo.

Only Rowena did not applaud. She sat with her hands folded in her lap, her nose elevated disdainfully. That angered her brother for he had heard her crying with the rest of the audience as Cleopatra had embraced death.

He had been so moved by the actress's performance that he was tempted to go backstage to deliver his compliments in person and pursue an acquaintance. Garth was deterred from doing so only by his strong disdain

13

for the rakes who haunted the greenrooms of theaters, seeking to buy the favors of ladies of the stage. He had no desire to be mistaken for one of that ilk.

Yet not only did he admire the little wasp's acting on stage, he had also enjoyed their sparring off stage. Her ire over his thinking her beneath him had surprised Garth. Surely she must know her place. Strolling players were virtual outcasts of society.

Indeed, he was more than a little shocked that he should be so attracted to such a woman. Never before had Garth had any inclination to select his feminine companions from the lower orders. He had not been tempted by even the most dazzling of the Cyprians and high-fliers who had tried to ensnare him.

Instead, he had been content to enjoy, in whatever capital he had been in, discreet liaisons with highborn ladies of various nationalities whose morals were as accommodating as their husbands were complaisant.

When at last the enthusiastic approval of the audience for the actress playing Cleopatra died away and the movement toward the exits began, Rowena complained to her brother about the nerve of the strolling players to charge so much admission.

In light of the stunning performance they had just seen, the modest admission had been a bargain. Rowena was so like their father, Garth thought bitterly. Sir Malcolm Taymor had never willingly spent a groat of his vast wealth except in pursuit of greater social status.

As they left the tent, Rowena said snidely, "These poor deluded yokels have no notion of what good acting is. When one has seen a great actress like Mrs. Siddons as I have, one can only marvel at their response to such an inferior performance."

Her unfair denigration of a fine performance outraged him.

"Stop making such a silly cake of yourself, Rowena! Everyone but you knows that we have seen an exceptional piece of acting. To contend otherwise is to proclaim yourself a fool."

Rowena, much miffed by this chastisement from her normally affable brother, stalked heavily to Garth's curricle, abandoning in her anger the small mincing steps that she thought was the proper gait for a genteel lady like herself.

They rode for nearly a mile back toward Tamar in silence before Rowena asked, "When shall I see dear Lady Serena?"

Garth wondered irritably when *he* would see her. He had been back in England for a month now and had yet to have so much as a glimpse of his betrothed. Through her brother, Thorley, now the Earl of Wycombe, she had refused all his pleas to call on her.

"Serena apparently is still suffering from the aftereffects of the measles." Garth did not believe this, but he did not tell his odious sister that he had a more sinister interpretation of his betrothed's lengthy illness.

As the weeks had passed without his being allowed to see her, he had become convinced that she had been stricken, not with the measles as her brother professed, but with the smallpox. This belief was strengthened when he learned that no one but Serena's sister-in-law and her maid were permitted in her sickroom for fear of spreading the contagion.

He wondered uneasily how cruelly that dread disease had ravaged her beauty. If his surmise about what was really wrong with Serena were true, it would painfully complicate his own schemes.

"You must set your wedding date as soon as possible," Rowena told him in her most nagging tone. "You know it was our father's dearest wish that you marry Lady Serena."

Sir Malcolm Taymor had regarded the betrothal he had arranged years ago of his young son and heir to the Earl of Wycombe's daughter as his greatest social triumph, even though such arranged marriages had fallen into disfavor.

Garth also knew that Rowena wanted the connection every bit as much as his late father had. Her own standing in society would be enhanced by having the daughter of an earl as her sister-in-law.

Rowena said, "You owe it to poor Papa, God rest his soul, to fulfill his most cherished desire. You were exceedingly cork-brained not to have wed Lady Serena when you were last home."

"I wanted her to have a London season first. It is such an important thing to a girl, and I feared that she would forever resent having been denied it."

Garth had had another, less noble reason for wishing his betrothed to have her season, but he was not about to confide that to anyone, least of all Rowena.

"It was very kind of you to be sure, but I pray you do not come to regret it. You must take care not to let her slip through your fingers."

If only he could be so fortunate.

The Walcott Strolling Players packed up their tent and set off down the road toward a country inn a few miles closer to their next destination, Toton Wells.

Sally Marlowe remained behind to catch a stage that would stop in Aveton the next morning on its way to Bath, where she would audition for the Theatre Royal.

Parting from her friends in the troupe was so painful for Sally that it brought tears to her eyes. In a burst of generosity that he could ill afford, Preston Walcott gave her as a farewell present her favorite garment—a cloak of midnight-blue velvet—from his company's wardrobe.

As Sally made her way alone down the main street of Aveton, she felt very elegant wrapped in her new cloak's softness. She was headed for the Crown and Scepter Inn where the coach would pick up passengers early on the morrow.

In one hand, she carried a shabby portmanteau that was stuffed with her meager belongings. Her other hand fingered the coins in her pocket that were her share of the proceeds from the performance of *Antony and Cleopatra*. She tried not to despair at how few were there.

Sally had been putting aside every ha'penny she could to help her parents. They had also been actors with the Walcott company until two months ago when her mama's ill health had forced them to seek refuge with Sally's older sister, who was married to a shopkeeper in Harrogate.

Poor Mama. Her dearest dream had been to retire to a cottage in the country, but she and Papa had not been able to save enough money to buy it. Now they were crowded into the cramped rooms over their son-in-law's small shop, and Sally feared that Mama would not live long enough to have the home she longed for.

Kindly Preston Walcott, knowing how desperately Sally wanted to help her mother, had urged the young actress to try out for the Bath Theatre Royal. If she were hired, she would receive a regular salary that would be much larger than what she could hope to earn under the best of circumstances as a strolling player.

Darkness was settling over Aveton, and the street was deserted except for a stout, middle-aged woman walking briskly toward her on the narrow street. Seeing Sally's face in the fading light, the woman suddenly curtsied to her respectfully, addressing her as Lady Serena.

Flattered at again being mistaken for an earl's progeny, Sally did not inform the woman of her error but acknowledged her greetings as gracefully as she thought a lady should.

Apparently the likeness must be every bit as strong as Lord Eldwin had said it was. Had that infuriatingly toplofty Corinthian outside the tent today thought Sally was the Lady Serena Keith, he would have bowed and scraped to her because he thought that she had the title "Lady" affixed to her name.

She wondered what he had thought of her performance. For some inexplicable reason, his opinion mattered to her. She had half-expected him to seek her out backstage afterward. Sally had recognized the sudden gleam of male interest in his eyes for what it was. She had seen it before, as a prelude to being offered an unwanted and unaccepted carte blanche. Growing up in the uninhibited world of the theater had revealed certain truths about mankind to Sally that would have shocked a more sheltered girl of her age.

She half-wished that he had made her such a proposition so she could have given him the set-down he deserved. Surely, she told herself, that was the only reason she had been disappointed when he had not visited her after the play.

It irritated Sally that she could not put the puffed-up creature from her mind. She tried to conjure up a set of circumstances in which she could achieve a sweet revenge that would bring him to his knees before her. But even her fertile imagination failed in this endeavor.

Sally passed an alehouse where boisterous male voices spilled out through the half-open door. A few steps beyond it an unattended gig waited in the street. Another half block brought her to Aveton's only inn, the Crown and Scepter, where she intended to spend the night.

This plan, however, was quickly thwarted by the establishment's dour proprietress. For a moment, the woman was fooled by the richness of Sally's velvet cloak into welcoming her. But then she noticed the girl's well-worn portmanteau, and her eyes narrowed suspiciously.

"Where is your maid and other baggage?" she demanded over the noise emanating from the inn's taproom next-door to the reception area.

When Sally admitted she had neither, the proprietress informed Sally with undisguised hostility that no woman traveling alone without her maid and a respectable amount of baggage would find shelter under her roof and that she must go elsewhere.

"There is no elsewhere," Sally protested. "This is the only inn in town. What am I to do?"

The woman, who was uniformly gray from the hair drawn severely up in a knot upon the top of her head to the hem of her cotton round gown, shrugged. "That is no concern of mine."

It was the second time that day that Sally had met with silly prejudice. She was exhausted and a little frightened to be alone in a strange town with no place to stay. Her anger flared, and in her intemperate outburst she let slip that she was an actress.

The proprietress instantly recoiled from Sally as though she were suffering from some deadly and highly contagious disease. In outraged accents, she announced that the Crown and Scepter would never disgrace itself by permitting actors, whom everyone knew were no better than rogues or thieves, to stay beneath its roof. Then she turned and marched indignantly off to the rear of the inn.

Wearily, Sally left. The last of the daylight had vanished while she was in the inn, and darkness gripped the town. Clouds concealed the moon and all but a few stars. She retraced her steps until she was abreast of the gig, still parked in the street. She paused beside it to consider what to do.

As she stood there, two young tulips of fashion, dressed to the nines in velvet with lace ruffles cascading from their wrists, staggered out of the inn's taproom toward the gig.

The taller of the jug-bitten pair, a bran-faced young man of perhaps two and twenty years with an ostentatious sapphire in the folds of his cravat, noticed her, and stopped in his unsteady tracks. He gave her a lascivious perusal that seemed to strip the very clothes from her body.

"What lovely morsel do we have here?"

"She looks like the little beauty I told you about," his companion said, "the one I saw this afternoon when I passed the strolling players outside of town."

Sally tried to brush past them, but the taller of the pair grabbed her arm.

"Not so fast, my pretty morsel." The odor of liquor

was heavy on his breath. "We know you're yearning to warm our beds tonight."

His companion smirked lecherously. "And to think, Jasper, we feared that we should have a dull night."

Although Sally was pluck to the backbone, she feared that they were too foxed for her to reason with them and that she was in grave danger. The so-called quality looked upon actresses as no better than whores and, therefore, fair game.

Thoroughly frightened now, she dropped her portmanteau and tried to break away from Jasper, but she was neither quick enough nor strong enough. He yanked her back with such force that she crashed against him. His other arm shot around her, trapping her.

"You're not going anywhere but with us, my lovely little wench," Jasper growled in her ear. "And don't think you will extort a handsome price from us for your services. You will take what we give you, and be happy for it."

Sally shuddered with hatred and revulsion. "Take your hands off me!"

"You will catch cold trying to act coy with us," her captor barked. One of his hands thrust through the front closure of her cloak to fondle her breast roughly. "We know you for what you are—an actress." The contempt in his voice left no doubt that he considered all females of her profession to be lightskirts.

It would be futile to inform him that he was dead wrong in her case and that her virtue was not for sale.

They would force her into the gig, dragging her off against her will. She was not nearly strong enough to fend off both of them. Nor, even if she could attract attention, would anyone be likely to help a lowly actress against two rich and fashionable young bucks.

Sally had only her wits to save her from becoming their plaything for the night.

3

Sally, fighting down her fear, recalled how closely she was supposed to resemble the Earl of Wycombe's sister. She seized upon this likeness as her only hope of outwitting her abductors.

Affecting the hauteur of an outraged lady of quality, she told them in her most cultured accents, "How dare you touch me! I am Lady Serena Keith. My brother, the Earl of Wycombe, will see you whipped for daring to lay a hand upon me."

Her claim provoked uncertainty in the randy young beaux. She felt the one holding her stiffen. The other said uneasily, "Lord Wycombe's home is very near here, Jasper. If what she says is true, there will be hell to pay. Perhaps we should let her go."

Jasper said sharply, "Don't be a pea-brain. She's merely trying to hoax us. The Earl of Wycombe's sister would not be walking alone down a village street."

His arms tightened around her, and he dragged her toward the gig. Sally screamed for help at the top of a voice that was used to filling theaters.

Her abductors were too foxed to silence her quickly, and four patrons from the alehouse rushed out.

She was certain that the real Lady Serena would fall into strong hysterics, and Sally obliged. She screamed that she was Lady Serena Keith and that she was being abducted.

In vain did Jasper and his friend protest that she was merely an actress.

"Me knows de Lady Serena when me sees 'er," said a big, burly man. "Take yer paws off 'er or me'll be polishing de cobbles with yer worthless carcass." He looked as though he would have no trouble carrying out his threat.

Jasper hastily released Sally, and she sidled out of his reach. His frightened companion tried to slip away, but one of the other men grabbed him roughly by the collar of his puce velvet coat and held him.

"Do not lay a hand on us." Jasper's attempt at bluster was negated by the quaver in his voice. "I shall have the magistrate upon you."

" 'Tis you e'll be wanting to deal with when 'e 'ears what you done to Lady Serena," was the ominous response.

Jasper visibly cringed. No one would much care what he did to an actress from a vagabond company of strolling players, but the attempted abduction of an earl's sister would be dealt with very harshly.

Sally continued to sob in feigned terror and shock. She was fully into the role of wronged lady of quality now, and she was playing it to the hilt.

"Methinks 'tis time to teach dese scoundrels not to be putting der filthy paws on de Lady Serena," the burly man said.

Sally had neatly turned the tables on her would-be abductors. Now they were the ones in danger. The fear on their faces told her that they both realized their peril.

Someone handed her a large, clean handkerchief, admonishing her to dry her tears.

A curricle approached at a lively pace, and a shout went up for it to halt.

"Most fortunate for you," one of Sally's rescuers told her kindly. " 'Ere be yer brother the earl now."

The wail she emitted at this news was genuine. She had been giving such a fine performance, and now his lordship would ruin it all by denouncing her as a fraud.

Nor could Sally suppress a tiny shiver of fear. She was terrified that when her rescuers learned that she was not Lady Serena, they would turn on her. She raged silently at the unfairness of the same woman being regarded so differently depending on whether or not she was thought to have the title of "lady" before her name.

Sally buried her face in the big handkerchief that she had been given. What with the handkerchief, the darkness, and all the confusion, perhaps the earl would fail to notice that she was an imposter until she could somehow make her escape.

The curricle, drawn by a matched pair of bays, clattered to a halt near the knot of people gathered in the street. Its lone occupant, a square-faced young man with unruly black hair and an impatient frown, jumped down.

Sally, who had never seen an earl, expected so lofty a personage to be somewhat stricken in years, and his youth surprised her into letting her hand holding the handkerchief slip away from her face.

The earl, who was still a good ten feet from her, exclaimed in amazement, "By God, it *is* you, Serena!"

Jasper groaned in frightened despair.

Sally hastily hid her face in the handkerchief again and dissolved into noisy sobs. Her only hope lay in keeping as much of her face as possible concealed behind the linen and pretending to be too hysterical to say anything coherent to his lordship.

Striding up to her, he clasped her arms. "What are you doing here, Serena?" he demanded roughly. "What the blazes has happened?"

She buried her face deeper in the handkerchief and sobbed all the louder.

"Why must you always be such a watering pot, Serena!" the earl exclaimed in exasperation. He turned to the other men. "What has happened to my sister?"

As they attempted to answer him, their attention was diverted from the two malefactors, who took advantage of this collective lapse to flee.

A shout went up, and the men from the alehouse ran after the escapees like a pack of hounds on the scent of a fox. Pursued and pursuers disappeared from sight around a corner, leaving Sally and Lord Wycombe alone in the street.

She was about to flee in the opposite direction when the earl grabbed her arm. "For God's sake, Serena, get in the curricle and let us be gone from here before that mob returns."

Since this was also Sally's most fervent wish, she grabbed her portmanteau and allowed the earl to hand her into his equipage. She would keep her face averted from him until they were well away from the scene. Then she would confess her deception and throw herself upon his mercy.

As the vehicle rumbled forward, the earl said, "I am excessively happy that you have finally come to your senses and returned. Where the devil have you been the past month?"

Sally was so startled by this query that she forgot to keep her face hidden. As she turned to stare at him, she recalled Sir Eldwin's skepticism about Lady Serena's protracted case of the measles.

"You cannot conceive the difficulty I have had fobbing Garth off all these weeks with tales of your being ill."

Wycombe sounded so profoundly harassed that Sally could not help but feel a little sorry for him, even if he was an earl.

Above them, the clouds were playing tag with the moon now, alternately revealing and obscuring it.

The earl said bitterly, "Had I any idea how long you would be gone, I should have told Garth that you were stricken with consumption rather than measles. If you do not want to marry him, Serena, you have to persuade him to cry off. Otherwise we will be ruined."

"Why?" Sally asked, momentarily forgetting in her surprise and curiosity the role she was playing.

"You damn well know why! I will be required to pay

back all the money that Garth's father loaned Papa on the understanding that you would marry his son. I have not the blunt to do that." He sounded truly desperate. "We stand to lose everything, even Wycombe Abbey, but if you get him to break the engagement, we are not obligated to repay the money."

Sally, her face carefully averted from him, listened to these revelations with fascination.

The curricle passed out of the village, leaving the murky outlines of its houses behind.

Sally asked a little nervously, "Where are we going?"

"Home, of course, you silly widgeon," Wycombe replied with asperity. "Where else would we be going?"

Sally had to tell him the truth about her identity. She was amazed that he had not tumbled to her deception by now.

Before she could speak, however, the earl demanded in deeply hurt accents, "Do you have any notion how much apprehension you have caused Emma and me since you ran away? Who have you been with this past month, Serena?"

Sally, remembering what Lord Eldwin had said, suspected that the answer might well be Lord Leland Caine, but she said only, "I do not know."

"How can you dare to say that you do not know? Good God, Serena, what has possessed you this past year?" A plaintive, almost pleading note crept into the earl's voice. "Why have you become so disobliging and sullen and spiteful toward your own family? What happened that day between you and Papa that turned you against us? You used to confide everything to me, poppet. Surely you can tell me?"

Sally turned to face him, confessing with a calmness she did not feel, "I cannot tell you because I am not your sister."

The clouds scudded away from the moon, and its

light revealed the face of a man whose patience had
been stretched beyond endurance.

"Stop trying to gammon me, Serena! You always
were a great one for making up stories, but this is outside of enough. Do you think that I don't know my own
sister, you maddening piece of baggage?"

Sally decided to adopt the accent that had been so
effective in convincing Lord Eldwin. " 'At's wot Oi
think, all right, for Oi ain't yer bloody Serena."

Wycombe gaped at her. "Good God, who the blazes
are you? Why were you pretending to be my sister?"

Sally told him who she was and how, after she had
been turned away from Aveton's only inn, she had been
accosted by the two drunken young fops.

When she confessed that she had pretended strong
hysterics because she had thought that would be the
way his sister would react, he actually laughed.

"How right you were. It is precisely the way Serena
would have responded. She dissolves into hysterics at
the smallest provocation."

His laughter eased her apprehension a little, and she
dared to ask, "Now that you know the truth, will you
stop your curricle and throw me into the night?"

After the way he had been hoaxed, she would not
blame him if he did. The equipage, however, had been
traveling through the night at a rapid pace. By now,
they were a considerable distance out of the village, and
Sally did not relish being abandoned in a dark and
lonely countryside that she did not know.

"I would not behave in such an abominable manner," he said gallantly. "If you will accompany me to
Wycombe Abbey, you can spend the night there."

Sally longed to accept this seemingly generous offer
but, having been raised in the theater, she was not so
green that she dared take it at face value.

Seeing the sharp, suspicious look she gave him, he
chuckled. "Do not fear that I have any design upon
your virtue. I am not in the petticoat line, and I have

no desire for any woman but my wife, Emma, who is awaiting me at the Abbey.''

He spoke of her with such warmth and love that Sally could not doubt his veracity, but she could not conceive that his Emma would be very pleased to have him bring home a young actress from a company of strolling players.

When she told him that, he replied, "My wife is the kindest hearted creature alive. When she hears your story, she will say I have done exactly the right thing."

Sally suspected he was overestimating Emma's amiability.

"I am astonished that you would take in such a lowly personage as myself," she said frankly.

"Oh, I am not at all caught up in my own consequence," he said cheerfully. "I do not hold with the notion that somehow an accident of birth makes me superior to my fellow men."

Sally had often espoused a similar sentiment, but she had never thought to hear it on the lips of an aristocrat who benefitted from this fiction.

The earl turned the curricle so quickly that Sally had to grab the edge of the seat to keep from being hurtled into him. They had left the road for a drive flanked by the dark silhouette of trees.

He said, "I like people for themselves, not their titles, and I like you. You are full of pluck." He gave her a small salute. "I applaud your quick wits in saving yourself from that despicable pair."

Sally had not expected to meet with such understanding and acceptance from a member of the quality, especially one of such exalted rank as an earl. He was the only swell she had ever met that she liked. How much nicer he was than that couple outside the tent. She wished that hatchet-faced woman and her infuriatingly toplofty companion could see her now, riding with an earl.

"You are most kind," Sally murmured. "I collect

that your sister ran away because she does not wish to wed her betrothed.''

"Yes, she disappeared the day after she learned that he had returned to England." He rubbed his hand wearily across his face. "She left us a note that she is hiding in a safe place where we will never find her and will not emerge from it until we publish a notice in the London papers announcing that her engagement is terminated.''

"Have you no idea where she is?''

"I am convinced that her bosom-bow, Netta Bridger, is hiding her, although the devious minx denies it," the earl said wrathfully. "In fact, I have no doubt that Netta concocted the entire scheme. Even if Serena were clever enough to have conceived it—and she is not—she would never have had the pluck to carry it out by herself.''

"So you are certain that she is with Netta?'' Sally asked, remembering what Lord Eldwin had said about Leland Caine.

"Yes. Were I not so certain I would be beside myself with worry." He shook his head despairingly. "Emma and I have often lamented that my sister is so much under Netta's influence. That female is as deceitful and calculating as she is clever. She never hesitates to employ underhanded means to attain her end, although what she thinks to gain from aiding Serena in this insanity is beyond me.''

"If your sister ran away a month ago, how have you managed to keep it a secret? Servants love to gossip about such things.''

"Only myself, Emma, and Serena's maid, Jane, know the truth. We have allowed no one else into the 'sickroom.' '' He paused, then added gloomily, "I don't know how much longer I can fob Garth off. He is cutting up stiff about not being allowed to see Serena.''

Although Sally sympathized with the earl's difficulties, she could not blame Serena for trying to escape

marriage to a man she disliked, and she bluntly told
Wycombe so.

"Most women would be delighted to have Sir Garth
Taymor as a husband," the earl said defensively. "Serena would have been quite happy to have married him
two years ago if only she could have had her come-out
first. Then she thought him exceedingly handsome and
charming."

"Why did she change her mind?"

"First, Netta convinced her that an earl's daughter
deserved better than a baronet's son for a husband. God,
how I rue the day my sister met that female! Second,
Garth has no notion how to handle Serena. I tried to
put a flea in his ear about holding the reins gently with
her, but I swear the nodcock did just the opposite. You
should see the letters that he wrote her from abroad.
Emma says they were hectoring enough to make any
woman cry off."

The veil of clouds had again rolled across the moon,
when the curricle stopped abruptly.

The earl said, "Welcome to Wycombe Abbey."

It was too dark for Sally to get much impression of
the earl's home, other than that it was a tall, bulky
building with dormers and a long flight of steps leading
up to the entrance. She had never before been privileged to enter a lord's house, and she was thankful for
her elegant velvet cloak.

The heavy doors were opened by a butler who so far
forgot himself when he saw Sally that he exclaimed in
shock, "Lady Serena!"

The butler's ejaculation was echoed by a slender
young woman whose lavender silk gown was in the first
stare of fashion. She had to be Emma. Her chestnut
hair was piled high on her head, and her lovely face
was dominated by a pair of warm brown eyes, so soft
and large that Sally was reminded of a doe that had
once come shyly up to her. The countess looked so
stricken at the sight of Sally that it appeared she might
faint on the spot.

Sally belatedly caught out of the corner of her eye a glimpse of another person in the hall, a man in russet riding coat, buckskin breeches, and highly polished boots, who was standing to the side of the door through which she had entered.

Wycombe also became aware of him, and he muttered a strangled expletive that Sally would never have expected to hear on the lips of anyone so high-bred as an earl.

The man in riding garb stepped forward and seized her hands roughly in his own.

''So, Serena,'' he said in a voice as cold as a north wind. ''At last I am permitted to see you.''

4

Sally, knowing that the man standing before her in rough possession of her hands must be Serena's betrothed, raised her head to inspect him.

Her heart seemed to stop for a moment, then resumed beating faster than it ought. For the second time that day, she was looking into a pair of emerald eyes framed by golden-brown lashes. Sally gasped in shock as she realized that Sir Garth Taymor was the man in the curricle who had so angered her earlier.

Now, however, his eyes were angry, not amused, and as hard as green granite. His lips were set in a thin, unsmiling line.

Sally was chilled by the change in him. Gone were his warm smile and mischievous, teasing manner. A shiver ran through her at what she read in his face.

She had been wrong earlier about one thing. Sir Garth was more inclined to murder the Lady Serena Keith than bow and scrape to her. He clearly disliked her as much as she did him.

Why, then, did he want to marry her?

Wycombe said weakly, "Garth, what a pleasant surprise."

"I doubt it," the visitor retorted sardonically, still examining Sally. "Do not look so overjoyed to see me again after our long separation, Serena."

He had not yet detected that Sally was not his be-

trothed. She was surprised that he had failed to notice
the resemblance between her and Lady Serena when he
had seen her earlier in the day. But, of course, she had
looked very different then with a black wig, ebony
brows, and darkened skin. And now she was wearing
an elegant blue velvet cloak that she was certain was
every bit as fine as any the real Serena possessed.

Garth studied her face intently as though searching
for blemishes on her pale, faultless skin.

Releasing her hands, he said, "Your severe illness
appears to have left no discernible mark upon you. Indeed, you look quite ravishing." The dry mockery in
his voice made it clear that this observation was not
tendered as a compliment.

Sally looked forward with malicious amusement to
the toplofty baronet's reaction when he learned that he
had mistaken an actress he considered so far beneath
his touch for his betrothed. That would teach him not
to be so high in the instep!

"Have you nothing to say to me, Serena?" he queried sharply.

"Only that you are mistaken. I am not S—"

"What *Serena* is trying to say," Wycombe broke in
hastily, "is that she is not scarred. Although her illness
has left no visible physical mark upon her, she is still
very weak from her long ordeal."

The earl had maneuvered himself into a position just
behind Garth's right shoulder, and now his dark eyes
desperately beseeched Sally not to contradict him.

She was astonished that he wanted her to pretend to
be his sister and beset by conflicting thoughts of what
she should do. It was not right to deceive Serena's betrothed. Yet the earl had been most kind to her, and
she liked him far better than the imperious Garth. She
could not bear to repay her beleaguered benefactor by
denouncing him as a liar.

Garth said scornfully to the earl, "I thought she was
about to insult my intelligence by attempting to deny
that she is Serena."

Sally's eyes narrowed angrily. So he would not even believe her if she tried to tell him the truth! Perhaps that was why Wycombe, suspecting as much, had stopped her from doing so. She asked in a provocative voice, "And you would never believe that, would you?"

"Not for a moment," Garth replied curtly. "So don't even try."

His brusque response settled the issue in Sally's mind. The overbearing bufflehead deserved to be deceived! She retorted acidly, "I would not dream of doing so."

She was rewarded by a look of profound gratitude in Wycombe's eyes.

"Surely a warmer welcome is in order from my betrothed after our long separation," Garth complained. "I believe a kiss is permissible."

Sally was so angry at him that she would sooner kiss a snake! "I . . . I may still be contagious," she lied.

"Very unlikely," he said icily. "In any event, as I have pointed out repeatedly the past month to your brother, I have already had the measles so you could not infect me."

Nevertheless, Garth made no move to claim her lips, and Sally suspected from his harsh expression that he did not particularly want to kiss her either. But if that were the case, why had he proposed it? Merely to irritate her?

Garth said with cold mockery, "As you walked in, Serena, your sister-in-law was explaining that you were too ill to see me."

The poor countess looked so mortified that Sally felt sorry for her. "You must not ring a peal over Emma, for it is all my fault." She spoke carefully, enunciating her words. A duchess could not have been more genteelly spoken. "I became so heartily sick of my room that I decided to sneak out for a bit of fresh air without telling anyone."

"So you have finally managed to overcome your freakish notion that fresh air is bad for you. It is good that you have, for as I told you it was a most nonsensical, pea-brained idea with which I had no patience.''

It struck her that he was deliberately trying to antagonize her, although she could not conceive why. However, if that was his aim, Sally was not going to rise to his bait.

When she said nothing, he looked disappointed. The wayward wave of golden-brown hair had tumbled down on his forehead again, giving him a boyish look that was incongruous with the hard set of his jaw and sensual mouth. Her breathing quickened. She longed to see his charming smile again.

He brushed impatiently at his hair, pushing it back from his face. ''Now, Serena, I will be private with you. We have much to discuss.''

Sally, unnerved by this prospect, said hastily, ''Oh, not tonight!''

His eyes narrowed. ''Why not?''

''I . . . I . . .'' As she floundered about for a plausible excuse, Garth looked as though he were enjoying her discomfort.

''Yes, tonight. I will not tolerate your setting your will against mine. I have made it very clear that my wife must be obedient to me. I am sorely out of patience with you.''

Repellent man! He sounded like a stern, unfeeling father chastising a young, not very bright child. It was enough to set Sally's teeth on edge, and she struggled to hang on to her temper. He was the most infuriating man she had ever met! No wonder Serena had run away rather than marry him. Sally would have done so too!

''I feel very faint,'' she told him in a deliberately shaky voice. She swayed a little as though she might indeed swoon. ''I fear I overdid my first outing.''

''Yes,'' Wycombe interjected quickly, putting his arms around her as though to support her. ''Ill as you have been, dear Serena, we cannot chance your suffering a relapse.'' He frowned at Garth. ''It is an odd time to be calling upon us. One does not expect uninvited visitors at such a late hour.''

Garth's eyes glimmered angrily at this rebuke. ''What else am I to do, since it is the only time that I can manage to see my betrothed?'' he asked sarcastically.

He turned to Sally, his lips set in an uncompromising line. ''I will call upon you tomorrow, Serena. We will talk then.''

Sally was still puzzled at the change in him from that afternoon. No one would suspect from his present conduct that he could be teasingly charming.

Even though he believed her to be his betrothed whom he had not seen for two years, he had not once smiled at her. Sally was certain that he did not like Serena. But if that were so, why would he want to go through with their marriage?

Or did he?

Could it be that perhaps *he* did not want to marry her and that he was trying to get *her* to break their betrothal?

Indeed, if that was his motive, then his behavior toward her tonight made perfect sense.

''Furthermore, Serena,'' Garth continued, ''you will accompany Emma and Thorley to the dinner I am having tomorrow at Tamar.''

''What if I do not?'' she challenged.

''You will, unless—'' His voice suddenly turned silky. ''—you wish to cry off from our engagement. Do you wish to do that, Serena?''

''No, of course, she does not!'' Wycombe inserted.

Had Sally not been observing Garth so closely, she would have missed the flash of disappointment in his eyes at Thorley's answer. It strengthened her suspicion that Garth was trying to goad Serena into ending their betrothal. Sally smothered an appreciative smile. He was more clever than she had given him credit for.

His green eyes examined her so intensely that her breath caught. ''I want to hear your sister's answer,

Wycombe. Do you wish to break our engagement, Serena?''

Sally's mischievous demon took possession of her,
and she could not resist saying adoringly, ''Garth, darling, I assure you that I do not wish to cry off.'' It was
even true, since she was not the one engaged to him.

She had to bite her lips to keep from laughing aloud
at his look of stunned dismay. At last, she had succeeded in turning the tables on this provoking man.

His eyes narrowed dangerously. ''I warn you, Serena, I will no longer be fobbed off with excuses of ill
health now that I have seen with my own eyes that you
are positively blooming.''

''Oh,'' Sally cooed sweetly, enjoying herself enor-
mously, ''do you really think I am blooming? How very
kind of you to compliment me.''

''I wasn't complimenting you,'' he said bluntly. ''I
must go now. You will see me tomorrow.''

''I can hardly wait,'' she said with a smile as dazzling as it was false.

He gave her an uneasy, searching look, trying to de-
cipher the reason for her sudden warmth toward him,
then turned on his heel and stalked to the door.

After Garth's departure, Wycombe quickly shep-
herded Sally and his wife into an antechamber off the
hall where no servants could overhear them. It was a
small but elegant room with eggshell-blue walls, white
plasterwork, and two rose settees.

The earl smiled at Sally. ''Thank you for going along
with me when I continued to let Garth think that you
were my sister.''

''I own I was not happy about doing so,'' she said
candidly, ''but after you pretended that I was Serena,
he would not have believed me if I had tried to tell him
differently.''

Emma stared at them as though they had both run
mad. ''Are . . . are you saying that she is not Serena?''
she asked her husband in disbelief.

''That's right. She is not my sister.''

From the stupefied look on Emma's face, it was clear that she was as amazed as her husband had been earlier. "They are astonishingly alike," she said weakly.

Wycombe said musingly, "Yes, the resemblance is uncanny."

"She even sounds like Serena," his wife observed.

"Not always," the earl said dryly.

"How old are you, Sally?" Emma asked.

"Nineteen."

"Same age as Serena," Wycombe said. "When is your birthday?"

"January 29th."

"Only two days after Serena's," Emma exclaimed. "But who are you?"

When the countess heard Sally's story, she proved that her husband's faith in her kindness was fully justified.

"But of course, you must stay with us!" she exclaimed without hesitation. "Such a dreadful experience."

Emma was so sympathetic that Sally was much touched. Despite the earl's faith in his wife's generosity, Sally had been convinced that no countess would take notice of a strolling player's plight.

A gilt-bronze clock on the marble mantel chimed the hour. Looking at it, Emma excused herself, telling her guest that it was her three-year-old son's bedtime and that she must go up to him as she did every night.

After Emma left, Sally turned to the earl and said, "Perhaps the situation with Sir Garth and Lady Serena is not as hopeless as you think. I suspect that he no more wants to marry your sister than she does him, although I cannot understand why he does not break the engagement."

"If you knew his family, you would not wonder! Such obnoxious social climbers. They would do anything for social advancement. I confess that I thought Garth cut from different cloth, but I fear I must have been wrong."

"But that cannot be it," Sally argued. "I do not believe that he desires the marriage either, but for some reason he wants her to be the one to end their betrothal."

Wycombe frowned. "Then it is the money! He is determined to force us to repay him, even though he is swimming in lard and will never miss it. As Garth grows older, I fear he is becoming as miserly as his father."

Sally had no sympathy for a man who would marry a woman he disliked merely for money he did not need. If he were that greedy, he deserved whatever he got.

Wycombe rubbed his hand wearily over his eyes. He looked so anxious and exhausted that her heart went out to him. The worried lines in his face were etched far too deeply for a man of his young years.

"Must Garth be the one to break the betrothal in order for you to escape the debt?"

Wycombe nodded, explaining that his late father, an extravagant and improvident man, had lived far beyond his means. He had turned to Garth's father, Sir Malcolm, a nip-farthing who did nothing that was not to his own advantage, to bail him out of financial difficulties. The elder Taymor, a notorious social climber who had long yearned for a connection between his family and the earl's, had agreed to help the beleaguered lord on condition that Serena, then a little girl, would wed Garth when she was emerged from the schoolroom. In exchange, all the money the earl borrowed and the sizable interest upon it would be forgiven when the engaged couple married.

If Serena, however, should break the betrothal for any reason, the notes would immediately become due and payable. If Garth were the one to do so, the debts would be forgiven.

"Why did you let Garth think that I was Serena?" Sally asked. "What will you tell him when he comes to see her tomorrow?"

Wycombe's gaze dropped from Sally's eyes. He said softly, "I am counting upon your assistance."

"What can I do?" she asked, surprised but willing to help him in any way that she could. She owed him that much for his kindness to her.

"Remain with us and continue to pretend to be Serena."

"What?" Sally gasped.

"You can save us from ruin by giving Garth such a disgust of Serena that he will break the engagement rather than wait for her to do so."

"You're out of your mind!" Sally cried with conviction. "How could I do that?"

Wycombe's face was suddenly flushed with excitement and hope. "Garth wants a wife who is demure, obedient, and genteel—a submissive model of decorum."

"How boring," Sally interjected scornfully.

"It's what most men want—can't blame him for that," the earl said defensively. "But if you pretend to be Serena and defy him, even shock him a little, show him that you are not at all the kind of wife he wants, he'll cry off quick enough."

"He will surely tumble to my being an impostor."

"I think not. He and Serena hardly know each other. He has been mostly gone from England since he joined the diplomatic corps nine years ago. When he last saw Serena, she was scarcely out of the schoolroom, and I have already warned him that she is much changed since that visit."

Sally asked herself whether she could continue to deceive that infuriating man about her identity. What an irresistable challenge to any actress, particularly one who thrived on difficult roles.

"It will take you no more than a sennight to get him to end the betrothal," the earl assured her with a cajoling smile. "We will announce its termination in the London papers, and Serena will come home."

"What if he realizes afterward that she's not the same woman?"

"I will see that he never gets close enough to her to do so. I'll put it about that she was so upset by his jilting her that she cannot bear to be in the same room with him. Oh, it shall be so easy if only you will agree to do it."

Sally was weakening. She liked the earl, and she would be happy to do anything she could to prevent his ruin.

And what a grand adventure for her to live as a lady of quality for a little while.

Furthermore, in her heart of hearts, Sally was inexplicably excited about the prospect of continuing to see Garth. Surely, she told herself, this was merely because she would enjoy watching him believe that a woman he considered so inferior to himself was his nobly-born betrothed. It would serve him right for being so high in the instep!

Still she hesitated.

"I will make it worth your while," the earl promised. "Five hundred pounds I will pay you."

Sally swallowed hard. That would mean she could make her mama's dream of a cottage in the country come true. She could not hope to earn such a sum in ten years of acting, and she desperately wanted Mama to have her home. The offer was so tempting. How could she refuse it?

Thorley gave Sally a beseeching look. "I beg of you to save us from ruin," he pleaded.

She battled with her conscience. After all, both parties to the betrothal clearly wanted it terminated, and she would only be ensuring that it was.

Who would be harmed in the end?

5

Sally awakened the next morning in the comfort of Serena's great featherbed tented with yards and yards of filmy green silk. She felt like the heroine of a fairy tale who had gone to bed a scullery maid and awakened a princess.

She had often dreamed of how wonderful the life of a lady of quality would be, cosseted from all the labors and cares of the world. And now she was living this dream, residing in a great country house. She had the luxury of a small fire, even though it was summer, to ward off the slight morning chill; her own maid to wait upon her; and the softest of beds to sleep in, rather than the straw pallet that was usually her lot. Serena's closet, larger than any room Sally had ever before inhabited, was jammed with elegant gowns in the first stare of fashion, all at her disposal.

Serena's abigail, Jane, a half dozen years older than her missing mistress, was clearly shocked by an impostor posing as her mistress, but she was too obedient a servant not to do as the Wycombes wished, and she agreed to aid the deception.

When Sally voiced concern that the other servants would become suspicious of her, Jane advised candidly, "You have only to ignore them as Lady Serena did. They've been careful to stay out of her way this past

year.'' Her tone unconsciously implied that she wished
she could have done so, too.

Sally tried to get Jane to tell her more about Serena,
but the maid was clearly unwilling to talk about her
mistress to a stranger and busied herself in laying out
a blue dimity round gown for Sally to wear.

After she donned it, Jane sat her down to dress her
golden locks.

''No need of a crimping iron for your hair. It is as
curly as milady's, and the same shade as well,'' Jane
marveled.

When the toilet was complete, Sally went over to a
full-length mirror on the wall between two tall, rect-
angular windows. They faced the east, and bright
morning sunlight streamed in upon Sally.

She clapped her hands in delight at the artful way the
maid had arranged her curls and threaded a blue satin
ribbon through them. When she complimented Jane on
her skill, the abigail seemed so startled and absurdly
pleased that Sally wondered whether Serena had ever
praised her.

The dimity gown the maid had chosen for Sally was
simply cut with a square neck and a soft, gathered skirt.
Its high empire waist was tied with a blue satin ribbon
that matched the one in her hair. She truly did look like
a young lady of quality.

Emma came into the bedchamber while Sally was
examining herself in the mirror.

When the earl had told his wife the previous night of
his plan to get Garth to cry off, she had been horrified
and had tried to dissuade him at first from his scheme.
But he had finally convinced her it was best for everyone involved, and she had reluctantly agreed to go along
with it.

The two women had stayed up late so that Emma
could coach the actress on various things that Serena
would know.

Sally had learned that Garth had been an envoy to
the court of Portugal in exile in Brazil. The death of

his father had brought him back prematurely to England. Garth had subsequently resigned from foreign service to oversee the vast estates he had inherited. It was the second great fortune that had been left to him. The first had come from his father's younger brother who had amassed it in India before he died there of typhoid.

Originally Serena and Garth were to have been married during his visit home two years ago after she had her London come-out season. The season had scarcely begun, however, when her mother had died unexpectedly. Since Serena could not appear in society during the mourning period, her season had been aborted almost before it had begun.

She had been disconsolate over being denied it. When Garth had returned home four months later, he had insisted their wedding be postponed so that she could have her season the following year.

Emma had observed to Sally, "I thought it exceedingly kind of him to do so, for his father was absolutely adamant that they be married immediately. Sir Malcolm Taymor was not an easy man to defy, and he flew into such a pelter, but Garth would not be budged."

Sally, who had been happy to think the worst of Serena's betrothed, had been a little shaken by the revelation that he could be compassionate. The scheme to hoax him went easier with her conscience when she thought him an arrogant pinch-purse, far too puffed up in his own consequence.

Now, as Emma wished Sally a good morning, she gave her a conspiratorial little smile. "I have come to take you down to breakfast, *Serena*. How are you today?"

"Nervous," Sally admitted. She was uneasy at how fragmented an impression she had of the girl she was pretending to be.

Although Emma had drilled Sally in a great many facts that Serena would know, her ladyship had been

evasive when Sally had tried to pin her down on her
sister-in-law's character.

Sally had only to gaze in the mirror to know what
Serena looked like, but her essence eluded the impostor.

"I confess I am nervous, too," Emma whispered,
studying Sally who was still standing by the mirror,
bathed in the sunshine pouring through the tall windows. "But I am comforted by the fact that even when
I see you in this strong light, you and Serena are as
alike as two peas in a pod. The likeness is astonishing."

"Do you truly think so, Lady Wycombe?" Sally
asked anxiously. Now that the moment was nearing to
launch the deception, it did not seem as easy to carry
off as it had the previous night, and she needed reassurance.

"You must not address me as Lady Wycombe," the
countess reminded Sally. "Remember, Serena calls me
Emma and my husband Thor. You must do the same."

There was so much to remember, Sally thought as
Emma guided her downstairs to the breakfast parlor.

The earl was already there, reading a London newspaper.

A large round table and a sideboard along one wall
dominated the room. A freckle-faced young footman in
a powdered wig and scarlet and gray livery was carrying a silver serving dish of broiled ham slices to the
sideboard. The delicious aromas of freshly baked
breads, coffee, tea, and bacon caused Sally's stomach
to protest convulsively her neglect of it.

Wycombe looked up from his paper and grinned at
her. "How nice to see you up and about again, Serena." He placed a slight ironic emphasis on the name.
"It has been a long time since we have had the pleasure
of your company at breakfast. Are you hungry this
morning?"

"Positively gut-foundered!" she exclaimed.

The footman gaped at her as though she had sprouted

a second mouth. The silver dish fell from his hands with a thud upon the sideboard and several pieces of ham slid from it, skidding to a stop against an arrangement of porcelain cups.

Emma was stricken into silence. Sally could think of nothing to say to cover her unfortunate lapse.

The earl came to her rescue, saying with feigned reproach, "I must again deplore the effect the London season has had on your vocabulary, Serena dear."

Sally, grateful for his help, said contritely, "I am sorry, Thor. I promise that I shall strive to be more careful."

"You don't know how relieved I am to hear that," he said dryly.

The footman, having restored order to both the sideboard and his shaken composure, hastily exited the room.

Sally, uncertain of what she was supposed to do, followed Emma to the sideboard. Her eyes widened at the feast that had been set out there: bowls of strawberries, custard, buttered eggs, and beefsteak pie; platters of cold salmon, bacon, broiled whiting and mackerel; plates of buttered eggs, muffins, and scones, and little bowls of marmalades and butter.

Never before had Sally seen such culinary largess. It would have fed the entire company of Walcott Strolling Players for a week.

She longed to heap her plate, but Emma took only small helpings from a few of the dishes and bypassed the rest. Sally reluctantly decided that she must follow suit.

At the table, she took Serena's place opposite the French doors that led to a rose arbor, abloom in pink and white and yellow. Beyond the roses, a graveled walk meandered through informally landscaped grounds sprinkled with oaks and beech and elms. In the distance a laburnum tree, dripping with golden flowers, topped a small knoll, like a dazzling crown.

As Sally ate, she looked longingly outside. It was

such a pretty day that perhaps the Wycombes would not mind if she took a walk later that morning. She shared her mother's love of the country. If Sally could live in such an idyllic spot as this, she would never leave it.

In a voice barely above a whisper, Thorley went over again the strategy that he had outlined to Sally the previous night: she should be forward, even bold, in feigning an eagerness to marry Garth while simultaneously doing all she could to give him a disgust of her. She had to convince him that if he did not want the marriage, he must be the one to end the engagement, that she would never cry off.

"Shock him," Thorley advised. "Show him that you are not the quiet, genteel pattern card of propriety that he wants for a wife. Also, Garth particularly detests bluestockings." The earl eyed Sally skeptically. "Would you be able to pretend to be one?"

Yes, she would, thanks to Mrs. Brinton, a wealthy invalid in Harrogate who had hired Sally to read to her each day.

The lonely chair-bound woman had catholic interests. Through her choice of books, she had introduced Sally to many subjects and had been quick to recognize her young companion's intelligence. Mrs. Brinton had loved to engage her in lively discussions that had sharpened Sally's wits. Indeed, she suspected that Mrs. Brinton had given her a better education than she would have obtained at the most select seminary for young ladies, where she would have learned more about deportment and embroidery than politics and philosophy.

Sally's employment with Mrs. Brinton lasted for three years, until her father lost his theater and the Marlowes were forced to join the Walcott troupe.

Although Sally did not doubt that she could impersonate a bluestocking, she questioned the wisdom of doing so.

"I am under the impression that your sister is something of a—er, featherhead. Won't Garth think it strange if—"

"He's been warned that Serena has changed so much he will hardly know her," Thorley said. "I'll tell him that was one of the changes. We've got to use every weapon we can. Garth was utterly repelled by Netta Bridger when she visited Serena while he was home two years ago. That odious bluestocking was embarrassingly persistent in seeking him out, trying to discuss politics and literature and heaven knows what else with him."

Sally wondered whether Thorley had considered the possibility that his sister might not be with her bosombow, but with Lord Leland Caine. "Are you certain that Netta is hiding Serena?"

"Of course," Thorley answered without hesitation. "Where else would she go?"

"Perhaps to Lord Leland Caine."

Emma gasped, and her hand holding her cup shook so that a little of the tea sloshed over the edge.

Her husband cried, "What the blazes do you know about Lee?"

"I heard gossip in Aveton that your sister seemed to prefer him to her betrothed." Sally saw no point in disclosing who had told her of Serena's *tendre*.

"Oh dear, has it become common knowledge?" Emma wailed. She turned to her husband. "What if Serena *is* with Lee?"

"Not even my sister could be so silly as to run off with that noddy," Thorley replied scathingly.

Emma looked unconvinced. "But he is such an excessively handsome noddy."

"I—" Thorley broke off hastily as the butler came in with word that Sir Garth had called to see Lady Serena and awaited her in the drawing room.

Butterflies took flight in Sally's stomach. Would she be able to continue to fool him into thinking she was his betrothed? Although she did not like Garth, she did not underestimate his intelligence. He might be arrogant and overbearing, but he was not stupid.

"It is very early to be calling," Emma said. "Shall I ask Garth to return this afternoon?"

"No," Sally preferred to face him now rather than later. What she was feeling was very similar to the pangs of stage fright that assailed her at the theater before she stepped on stage to face a new audience. Better to get it over with.

Thorley grasped her hand and gave it a reassuring squeeze. "Now remember, give Garth a disgust of you."

As Sally approached the drawing room, disconnected bits and pieces of what she had been told about Serena floated in her mind. She hoped that she could keep it all straight.

In the drawing room, Garth was sitting on a green plush settee. His head was turned toward the long windows overlooking the formal garden, and he did not notice Sally come in.

Studying his profile, she was struck again by how handsome he was with his wavy golden-brown hair, straight, noble nose, and strong jaw. She tried to tell herself it was her deception, not the man himself, that was responsible for the way her pulse accelerated alarmingly at the sight of him.

Garth belatedly glanced around and saw her. He jumped up from the settee, exclaiming, "Serena!"

His astonished expression told Sally that he had not expected her to appear. The icy anger of the previous night was gone from his eyes, replaced by a slightly bewildered look that she found disconcertingly appealing.

She gave him an innocent smile. "Why are you so surprised to see me? Did you not ask for me?"

"Yes, but I thought you would try again to fob me off, just as you have for weeks," he said bluntly.

"You do me a grave injustice to think I do not want to see you," she assured him. "I own, however, it is an unusually early hour to be calling."

"But the early bird gets the lady's company, does he

not?'' he asked sardonically. ''When I call at more conventional hours, I am turned away.''

It was time to launch her campaign to make him believe she was eager to marry him. Batting her eyes flirtatiously, she said, ''I promise you now that I am recovered from my illness, I shall be delighted to see you whenever you call, dearest Garth.''

He did not look at all pleased by this reassurance.

''What a clanker,'' he scoffed. ''I am persuaded that like Portia with her suitors in *The Merchant of Venice*, you dote on my absence.''

He was not easily hoaxed, Sally thought uneasily. She gave him a boldly admiring look. ''But, dearest Garth, that was only because I had forgotten how handsome you are.''

It was all she could do to keep from laughing aloud at the shock on his face. For a moment, he only stared at her. Then he said coldly, ''Next you'll be telling me the earth is flat.''

She could not resist retorting mischievously, ''Not entirely flat. It is quite mountainous in places like the Alps.''

He looked perplexed, as though he could not believe that she could be teasing him. Then he said abruptly, ''It is far too beautiful a day to remain inside, is it not?''

His provocative tone puzzled her. If he expected her to argue the point, he was disappointed for she immediately agreed with him.

''Do you prefer a horseback ride in the park or a walk in the garden?'' he inquired.

Sally was discomforted by this unexpected choice. She had gathered that Serena was indolent and, therefore, would most likely choose to ride rather than walk. Sally dared not do so, however, for she had never learned to ride sidesaddle. This ignorance of a skill that Serena would surely possess might well betray her.

So she said, ''Please, I prefer to walk.'' She gestured toward the windows that looked out over the informal garden beyond the rose arbor. "Indeed, I was thinking at breakfast how much I should enjoy strolling along that path among the trees."

For some reason, this seemed to astonish him, but he said only, "Then get your bonnet and parasol."

Sally wanted neither item, preferring instead to let the sun warm her face. She collected, however, that Serena would not go out without them, and she dutifully went to fetch them.

As she did, he said sternly, "Do not keep me waiting."

"Oh, I shan't, I promise." Sally flashed him an adoring smile. "I enjoy your company too much."

She was rewarded by a look of mingled suspicion and alarm that made her all the more certain Garth wanted to end the betrothal as much as Serena did.

As Sally hastened upstairs, she was a little disconcerted at how excited she was by the prospect of walking with Garth. Surely, it was only because she savored the challenge of duping him, wasn't it?

When she told Serena's abigail what she needed, Jane first brought from Serena's closet a black redingote edged in blue.

"I don't need that," Sally said as the maid thrust the garment into her hands, "only a bonnet and parasol."

"Lady Serena would not dream of going outside without a coat. Her health is too delicate. Indeed, she avoided the outdoors whenever possible."

"So you have finally managed to overcome your freakish notion that fresh air is bad for you." That comment of Garth's the previous night now made more sense to Sally.

Jane disappeared back into the closet to find a suitable hat and parasol.

Sally tried on the redingote. It was too heavy for such a warm day as this, and she could not bear to wear it no matter what Serena would have done.

Nevertheless, it was a lovely garment, and Sally strode over to the full-length mirror in a gilt frame to see how she looked in it. As she eyed herself in the glass, she pushed her hands into its pockets, and her fingers closed upon a paper stuffed in one of them.

Pulling it out, she discovered it was a single-page letter to Serena from Garth while he had been in Brazil. Curiosity was Sally's besetting sin, and she could not resist skimming through it to see what he had written to his betrothed.

It seemed full of dubious advice. He recommended the importance of her employing drastic means—such as cold baths in an icy creek—to harden her fragile constitution.

More likely it would kill the delicate Serena! Sally thought angrily. But perhaps that was what he wanted!

Another paragraph caught her eye: "You mentioned you were reading *The Mysteries of Udolpho*. You must take care that you do not become a bluestocking."

As though reading that Gothic confection could signify an elevated mind, Sally thought scornfully, stuffing the letter back into the pocket of the redingote. The odious man must want a wife as ignorant and unread as she was meek.

The letter confirmed what Thorley had said about Garth's dislike of bluestockings. Putting the redingote aside, Sally smiled mischievously as she considered the tactics she would employ to provoke him into crying off.

6

With suspicious eyes, Garth watched his betrothed leave the drawing room to get her bonnet and parasol. What kind of game was the little minx playing with him?

He sank back on the green plush settee. The change in her since he was last home two years ago confounded him. That previous visit had been his first exposure to Serena since she had emerged from the schoolroom. At first, Garth had been well pleased by the brilliant match that his father had arranged for him. Not only was Serena an earl's daughter, but she was a rare beauty, delicate and ethereal, with the pretty manners and graceful bearing of a young lady of quality.

He had been raised with the assumption, prevalent among men of his class, that matrimony was more business than romance. An advantageous union, not love, was the first priority, and marriage to an earl's daughter was certainly that. Garth had counted himself fortunate that Serena was a demure, eye-stopping beauty in the bargain.

Having never been passionately in love, he had only a rather vague notion of what he wanted his wife to be like. Indeed, he knew better what he did not want in her than what he did. No prattle-box for him, no bold flirt who would later prove unfaithful, no hoyden who mortified him with her antics, no bookish bluestocking who set her views against his, no managing female who would try to make him dance to her tune. He had no intention of living under the cat's paw.

He had been relieved to discover that Serena was none of those things. Despite her beauty, she was not flirtatious. Nor bookish or hoydenish either. She was so demure that she bordered on the timid. Serena also seemed blessed with excellent good sense for she always listened quietly to him, never interrupting and readily agreeing with all his opinions. Nothing could be more repugnant than an overbearing female who challenged his views or his authority.

Initially he had been so well pleased with Serena that he had even told Thorley that she was just the kind of quiet, guileless, well-behaved girl that he had dreamed of marrying.

By the time that visit was a month old, however, he was beset by a nebulous but growing unease. Serena's company and even her beauty began to pall. Only the most commonplace utterances issued from her lovely little mouth. She was incapable of conversing on any subject other than herself, her clothes, and parties. Garth doubted that she had ever read a book out of curiosity or for pleasure. Her acceptance of his views stemmed from ignorance and indifference rather than a compatibility of minds.

Lovely as her face was, it possessed no more animation or vitality than her mind. Her distressing tendency to dissolve into hysterics at the smallest provocation irritated him. An innocent moth alighting on her dress was enough to set her off. He could not admire such a fainthearted creature.

She was also selfish. Garth had been profoundly shocked to discover that she acted far more distressed by the sudden curtailment of her London season than by her mother's death that had necessitated it.

Honor, however, did not permit a gentleman of good breeding to cry off from a betrothal, particularly one of such long standing, and Garth was very much a gentleman. A woman could jilt her betrothed with impunity, but if he were to do so he would be branded a cad.

Desperately, he had seized upon Serena's complaints of having been denied her come-out as an excuse to postpone their wedding. He even secretly promised her reluctant father that he would bear the expense for her season. Garth did so in the ardent hope that she would fall in love with one of the suitable young men she would meet during it and cry off.

To his acute disappointment, never once during the next two years did her boring epistles to him offer the smallest indication that she was developing a *tendre* for any other man.

London society did, however, inflate her marital expectations. The ninnyhammer did not disguise that she had come to think it beneath her, the daughter of an earl, to marry the son of a mere baronet, no matter how rich. Garth was stung by her shallow measure of him.

When he returned home from Brazil, he was determined to get her to break their betrothal. He would exploit to the fullest her irritating belief that he was unworthy of her hand. But his campaign was immediately stymied because he was not allowed in her presence.

He became so convinced that she must be suffering from the smallpox that when he finally did see her the previous night, his first reaction was enormous relief that she bore no visible scars. Had she been badly disfigured by that dread disease, any hope of her attracting another suitor would have been dead, and he would be stuck with her.

It had not taken him very many more minutes, however, to conclude that she had not been ill at all—that it had merely been an excuse to escape his company. Her shock and dismay when he had seized her hands had encouraged his hope that he could spur her into crying off, freeing them both from what would surely be an intolerable union.

Yet now she was acting as though she was delighted with him. It made absolutely no sense. He would have thought she was hoaxing him except that the Serena of two years ago would not have known how. Lacking both wit and levity herself, she had never been able to recognize either his humor or his teasing for what it was.

Garth, hearing the rustle of petticoats at the drawing-room door, looked up. His betrothed was standing there, and all other thoughts were banished by the sight.

Her exquisite face was framed most becomingly by a poke bonnet tied beneath her ear with wide blue satin ribbons that matched her dress. She twirled a blue parasol in one dainty hand. A charming smile graced her lips, and her blue eyes sparkled with an impishness that he had not seen in them before. He thought admiringly that she looked as though she had just stepped out of a particularly flattering Gainsborough portrait.

Never before had she looked so lovely to him.

Nor so tempting! He felt his body's helpless response to her provocative charm.

Good God, had he taken leave of his senses? He knew what Serena was. How could he suddenly yearn to hold her in his arms?

Much disturbed, he led her outside.

She said with more liveliness in her voice than he had heretofore heard, "I am so pleased that you wanted to walk."

Her sudden eagerness for this activity astonished him. Two years ago all exertion had been repugnant to Serena. When he had insisted upon just such a walk as she professed to want today, she had complained vehemently that the exercise would give her ugly muscles and the sun would ruin her skin.

He had learned during that outing that Serena's ignorance of nature was profound. She had told him pettishly that she had no interest in learning to tell one boring bush, bird, or tree from another.

Garth had been dismayed. He had a deep and abiding love for all things green and growing that he had hoped his future wife would share. To him, one of the great pleasures of living in foreign lands had been seeing flora that was unknown in England, but when he tried to tell Serena about them, she yawned and changed the subject.

Now, Garth guided her toward the rose arbor before she could change her mind about walking. Once they were well away from the house, he would strive to irritate her by talking about the boring bushes and birds they would be observing.

As they passed among the roses, Serena bent over a fragrant white bloom. He could not help admiring her blonde beauty and petite form. Her skin was as pale and soft as the petals of the rose she was admiring. She looked beguilingly sweet and innocent as she breathed in the flower's perfume.

Garth wished wistfully that her mind was half so lovely as her face. But he had no hope that Serena had used the past two years to improve her knowledge of the world. Indeed, only once in her letters to him had she mentioned reading a book—*The Mysteries of Udolpho*. He had not been able to resist writing back with savage sarcasm that she must take care not to become a bluestocking.

They left the arbor and walked along the path that undulated through the oaks and elms and beech.

As they neared the laburnum, Garth cast a sidelong glance at his betrothed. She was staring with an appreciative smile, her eyes as bright and blue as forget-me-nots, at the tree's brilliant yellow cascade of flowers.

He remarked idly, "Easy to see why they call it the tree of golden rain."

"Yes," she agreed. "So beautiful and so poisonous. It must be a Scotch laburnum to be still in flower this late. The Scotch variety blossoms two or three weeks after the common one."

His head spun around in surprise that a shatterbrain previously so ignorant of nature should know the difference.

She left the path and strode briskly over to the tree. There was a lightness and eagerness to her step that bespoke an enthusiasm and energy that were not there two years ago. She reminded him of a graceful wood sprite.

After examining the laburnum's leaves, she announced, "It is a Scotch as I thought."

Could it be, he wondered, that she had made an attempt to please him by learning more about the natural world around her? "How is it that you know the difference?"

She broke off a sprig of three leaflets and held it out to him. "You see these leaves on the Scotch are larger and hairless," she explained earnestly. "The others have smaller leaves with silky white hairs on the underside."

"No, no," he said impatiently. "I mean how is it that *you* came to learn the difference between them."

She looked at him as though he were queer in the attic. "What an odd question. Why should I not?" The angry edge to her voice was unmistakable. "Are you one of those Gothic men who think women should confine their interest only to gossip and embroidery?"

"I admire an inquisitive mind, whether it be in a man or a woman," he retorted. If only she possessed one! "Are you telling me you have developed interests beyond your clothes and parties?"

Her eyes flashed like blue fire. "I am not the widgeon you clearly think me!"

If only that were true, Garth thought unhappily.

They returned to the gravel walk. Thinking to bore her, he began telling her about some of the strange trees, unknown in England, that he had seen during his years abroad. Again she surprised him by exhibiting what was obviously a genuine interest.

Suddenly, she sighted a columbine in bloom and darted off to inspect its drooping bell-like blue flowers.

She looked so fragile, so ethereal, and moved with

such lightness and grace that Garth was again reminded of an enchanting wood sprite.

When she returned to him, he said, "I collect you have become a nature lover, sprite."

"Why do you call me that?"

He smiled. "Because you remind me of a wood sprite."

As they continued along the path, he described to her his favorite exotic tree, the jacaranda of Brazil with its lacy, fernlike leaves and showy drops of purple flowers.

She exclaimed enthusiastically, "How beautiful it sounds. I should so like to see one."

She even managed to sound like she meant it.

More astonishing, Garth did not see in her blue eyes the dull and disinterested gaze he remembered; they were brilliant with a vivacity that he had not thought she possessed.

And what a delightful, enticing mouth she had. He was unnerved by the sudden urge he had to kiss it.

And baffled. Not until today had he felt such a strong desire to touch her.

Much shaken, Garth wavered in his determination to provoke her into ending their betrothal.

But he vacillated only for a moment. Skeptical that anyone could change as much as Serena seemed to have, he feared that he would again find himself as disillusioned by her as he had been two years ago.

Garth plotted his strategy. First, he would give her an opportunity to break off the engagement. If that failed, he would turn her ridiculous belief that she was superior to him to his advantage.

He laid a light hand on her arm. "Stay a minute, Sprite."

An odd shiver went through Sally at his touch.

Garth led her to a bench that had been placed along the path beneath the shade of a holly oak.

When they were seated, she turned her face toward his. His green eyes, fringed by his thick golden-brown lashes, studied her with a grave intensity that caused Sally's heart to skip erratically. A strange excitement coursed through her.

"Serena, I desire that there be only honesty and plain dealing between us. We are in a deucedly awkward position. You were still a child when I embarked upon my diplomatic travels. We are little more than strangers to each other. Yet, thanks to our fathers, we are engaged."

His eyes were sincerely troubled now, and Sally felt a rush of sympathy for him as he summed up his and Serena's dilemma.

"I am not at all persuaded, Sprite, that marriage to me is what you want."

"Why . . . why would you think that?" Sally asked.

"I believe you consider it beneath you, an earl's daughter, to marry me."

Sally was startled by his perception. Thorley had told her that was precisely what Serena thought.

Suddenly, the irony of the situation struck Sally. Yesterday it had been Garth who had told her how far beneath him she was, and now she had the opportunity to pay him back in kind. It was all she could do to suppress her amusement as she solemnly agreed, "Yes, you are." She could not resist adding, "Very far beneath."

Let him see how he liked the shoe now that it was on the other foot!

From the flash of anger in his eyes, he did not like it at all. Instead of responding hotly, however, he surprised her by saying sympathetically, "I understand why you feel that way, Serena. I know I must seem only half-respectable to one of a family as old and proud as yours."

Sally was amazed that a man as high in the instep as he could bring himself to make such an admission.

"Not only am I a mere baronet," he continued dolefully, "but, of course, my fortune is tainted."

That shocked her into exclaiming, "Tainted? By blood?"

"No, worse," he said tragically. "By trade."

Sally blinked in surprise. She had heard that swells held queer notions about what kind of fortunes were acceptable to society, but she thought such ideas nonsense. So long as it was honestly earned, blunt was blunt.

"You know that my uncle, the one who died a dozen years ago and left me my first fortune, was nothing but a nabob," Garth said, desperate to exploit anything that might strengthen Serena's aversion for his family. To his dismay, she did not blink at this revelation. He continued in the tone of a man revealing a terrible skeleton in his closet. "My grandfather was a mere ship owner."

Actually, he had owned a very large fleet of ships, numerous warehouses, and a lucrative international trading business, but Garth, intent upon increasing his betrothed's disgust, wished to downplay his forebear's successes. He chose not to remind her that his mother's father had been a viscount. Nor that he numbered an ambassador, a former chancellor of the exchequer, and a deputy foreign secretary among his maternal relatives.

Rushing his fences, Garth said, "I can understand why you would not want to marry into such a family as mine."

She shrugged. "Better to come by your blunt in an honorable trade than by starving your unfortunate tenants as some aristocratic landlords do."

Garth looked at her in dismay. While he agreed with her, it was definitely not the sentiment he expected— or wanted—to hear from her lovely lips.

He thought ruefully that she was accepting the suspect origins of his fortune with more equanimity than his father had. Sir Malcolm had devoted his life to trying to rise above the stigma of trade while simultaneously multiplying his financial worth. He had been far more successful in the latter endeavor than the former.

In desperation, Garth abandoned any pretense of the honesty and plain dealing he had said he wanted between them. "I fear, Sprite, that in my grandfather's case it was not even an honorable trade."

That got her attention. "Why?"

"I am convinced he was a pirate," Garth replied, shamelessly sacrificing his straitlaced progenitor's heretofore spotless reputation.

He then proceeded to graft onto his family tree an appalling assortment of imaginary thatch-gallows, knights of the road, and even a common cutpurse.

To his mingled surprise and unhappiness, she seemed more fascinated and amused than repelled by his newly invented ancestors. She asked him so many questions about them that his ingenuity was severely taxed to come up with appropriately repugnant details and ominous nicknames. His fictitious additions included Cutthroat Charlie, a highwayman who earned his sobriquet from his method of dispatching his victims, and Pegleg Pete, a pirate who had been the terror of the Atlantic.

Finally, Garth said in the most humble tone he could command, "If you wish to cry off, I will understand. As you yourself said, marriage to me is too far beneath you."

"Yes, of course it is," she said cheerfully, maliciously agreeing with him, "but you need never fear that I will ever break our betrothal."

It was all Sally could do to hide her amusement at his consternation. She had guessed early on the real intent of his fraudulent revelations about his family. She admired the cleverness of his tactic, suspecting that it would have been highly effective with the real Serena.

Sally was certain now that Garth was every bit as determined to get her to break the betrothal as she was to get him to do so. She would enjoy matching wits with him. He was a challenge worthy of her.

Indeed, Sally had been so entertained by his creative, and often funny, storytelling that she found her dislike of him fading. She tried to stifle the growing attraction that she felt for him. Hastily, she reminded herself of how he had so unjustly denigrated the Walcott Strolling Players in general and herself in particular the previous day.

Even then, though, she had difficulty hardening her heart against him. She was amazed that a man of his pride could create such a scandalous set of forebears for himself. He had a far livelier sense of humor than she had suspected, and she was charmed by it. And by the mischievous gleam in his green eyes.

Sally wondered why he was so desperate to escape marriage to Serena. And since he was, why the devil did he not cry off himself?

It was the money, of course! Thorley had said Garth was becoming as clutch-fisted as his father. He wanted Serena to be the one to break their engagement so that all the blunt the late earl had borrowed would have to be repaid.

Sally's rising opinion of Garth plummeted. Such a muckworm as that deserved to be hoaxed, she told herself sternly.

He rose from the oak bench and helped her to her feet. As they started back toward Wycombe Abbey, he suddenly asked, "What is the real reason I have not been permitted to see you the past month? You are far too healthy for me to believe that you have been so ill."

"I . . . I could not bear for you to see me until I was looking my best," Sally improvised hastily.

"Are you certain that it was not because you neither wanted to see me nor to marry me? I beg of you, Sprite, be honest with me."

She was moved by his plea, but honest was one thing she could not be with him.

When she said nothing, he quoted sadly:

"For what is wedlock forced, but a hell,
"An age of discord and continual strife?"

Sally, recognizing the lines from Part I of Shakespeare's *Henry VI*, completed the quotation:

"Whereas the contrary bringeth bliss,
"And is a pattern of celestial peace."

He stopped dead in the path and gaped at her much as the footman had done that morning in the breakfast parlor, but Sally could not fathom what she had said wrong this time. She knew that she had remembered the lines correctly. "Why do you look at me so strangely?"

"I am astonished at how accurately you can quote from that relatively obscure play. How do you know the lines so well?"

The play was part of the Walcott Strolling Players' repertoire. They rarely performed it, but when they did, Sally appeared as Joan of Arc. She could not, however, tell him that. Instead, she gave him a guilty little smile and said in the tone of one confiding a mortifying failing, "I fear that you have discovered my dreadful secret—I have bookish tendencies."

"You do?" His voice betrayed strong skepticism.

"Yes," she assured him.

"You must be very bookish indeed to recall the lines of that particular play so well," he said dryly.

"I . . . I daresay I remembered the passage because it seemed to me to be so true."

His thick golden-brown brows knit in a puzzled frown. "Yet you are willing to enter into just such a forced marriage as it warns against. For God's sake, Sprite, if you wish to cry off, I will understand."

Sally wanted to groan in frustration at his insistence she be the one to break their betrothal. "I told you before that I will never do so. If you wish our engagement ended, it must be you who severs it."

Garth looked genuinely horrified. "Good God,

Sprite, you know that I cannot do that!'' he cried in shocked accents.

Was the money that important to him, Sally wondered angrily. If he was such a nip-cheese that he would wed a woman he did not want rather than forfeit what the Wycombes owed him, he deserved a miserable marriage!

Garth's green eyes studied her with probing intensity. ''Why do you want to marry me, Serena?''

It was the perfect opportunity for Sally to follow Thorley's instructions to give Garth a disgust of her.

She answered with all the coldness she could muster, ''You are exceedingly rich.''

7

Garth jerked back as though his betrothed had slapped him. "I said that I wanted honesty and plain dealing between us," he said sardonically, "and now I collect that you are giving it to me."

Her challenging gaze met his. "Was it honesty that impelled you to tell me those Banbury tales about your nonexistent relatives, Cutthroat Charlie and Peg-leg Pete?"

At least, Garth thought, she was no longer the green, gullible girl who, to his extreme annoyance, had taken everything he said with absolute seriousness. He wondered at what point today she had tumbled to the fact he was falsifying his family history. The Serena of two years ago never would have.

That was small comfort, however, in light of his affianced's blithe admission that she was no better than a female fortune hunter. Garth was still reeling from the shock of that. Until today, he had thought Serena many things: colorless, shallow, spoiled, timid, humorless, and—above all—boring. But not greedy.

In his agitation, he unconsciously resumed walking back toward Wycombe Abbey. To Garth's eye, the house had always seemed alien to the green Kent landscape. Its hipped roof, dormers, and modillion cornices looked more Dutch than English.

The second earl, a Royalist, had fled to Holland when

Cromwell seized power, where he had grown fond of the architecture. He had borrowed heavily from it when, after his return from exile, he had built his country home on the ruins of an old abbey.

Garth's betrothed fell into step beside him on the path. He cast her a venomous glance. Damn her, but she had him between a rock and a hard place.

Serena knew as well as he did that no man of honor could end his betrothal. To polite society, jilting her would be almost as despicable as seducing and abandoning her. The minx was trying to force him to choose between a disastrous marriage or being branded a cad and social pariah by the high sticklers of the *ton*.

He shook his head incredulously. Didn't the little fool realize that her future happiness, as well as his, was at stake? "Do you truly mean that you are marrying me only for my fortune?"

"Of course," she replied calmly.

Garth stopped abruptly. Seizing her arm, he forced her to face him.

She looked up at him with wide-eyed innocence. "What other reason could I have?"

Beset by outraged feelings of ill usage in general and wounded pride in particular, he said acidly, "I am generally held to be good company. Most ladies do not find me repugnant to the eye. I won't scruple to tell you that your motive shocks me."

"Pooh, yours is no better than mine. You agreed to marry me only because I am an earl's daughter, and you wanted the connection to my family."

"That's not true," he cried in more haste than truth. Then his conscience assailed him.

"What other reason could you possibly have for wanting to marry me?" she demanded.

Garth could scarcely believe that Serena, whom he had dismissed as a meek, silly slowtop, was confronting him like this. The diplomat in him knew that he should praise her beauty and breeding and whatever other of her meager accomplishments he could think of, but he was so angry that the truth spilled from his lips before he could stop it.

"Dammit, I do not want to marry you at all!"

"Ah," she said triumphantly, "honesty and plain dealing at last."

For the first time in his life, Garth thought he might actually be capable of hitting a woman. Then his own innate honesty forced him to acknowledge that he had deserved her thrust.

She said coolly, "If you did not want to marry me, you should not have agreed to do so all those years ago."

"But I did want to then." That was true. Garth had been too young and green to suspect that it would not be the perfect match his father insisted it would be. Serena had been such a taking little girl, and Garth had wrongly assumed that she would grow up to be like her gentle, loving mother, whom he had revered. Instead, she had grown up to be very different.

He said, "When our fathers made that agreement, we were both too young to understand that we would change as we grew up and, as adults, would not suit."

Garth perceived from her face that he had scored a point, and he hastened to add what he believed was his most effective argument. "You admit that you think marrying me is beneath you. I am persuaded that happiness is not possible between two people who do not hold each other in mutual respect."

Although Sally concurred with him, she could not resist retorting, "But I respect your fortune, and I am persuaded it and I are well suited."

Garth cried in frustration, "For God's sake, wealth does not ensure happiness. If that is why you are marrying me, I beg of you to cry off."

"*You* cry off! It is *you* who does not want to wed *me!*"

"How can I if your only reason for marrying me is my fortune?" he asked, not unreasonably.

"You did not want to marry me even before I told you that."

"I have never said anything to indicate that was the case."

"Actions speak louder than words!"

"What actions? I have not even been allowed to see you for the past month. For some reason, I have been fobbed off with flummery about the measles."

Gazing into his green eyes with their expression of mingled hurt and anger, Sally felt a sympathy for him that was hard to stifle. Looking at the situation from his perspective, she had to admit he had good reason to be upset with his betrothed.

"Listen to me, Serena," he said with quiet sincerity. "Any woman who lets a man's fortune outweigh all other considerations is a fool."

Sally agreed, but she could not admit it to him. Instead, she said defiantly, "Then I am a fool."

They resumed walking down the undulating path toward Wycombe Abbey in strained silence. As they passed the golden laburnum tree, she challenged him, "Why do you not want to marry me?"

Garth longed to blister her ears with all his reasons, but he controlled the spleen threatening to burst forth. It was time to play the only card that he had left, and he must do so diplomatically.

"Serena," he said with a gentleness he was far from feeling, "my fear arises as much from my concern for your future happiness as for my own. We are so very different. You love London and parties. I love the country and solitude."

Garth also liked London society, but in his efforts to get her to cry off, he had written her with premeditated mendacity that they would live a reclusive life in the country, never visiting the capital.

He said sternly, "When we are married, you must give up London." He was certain that she would sooner cut off her arm.

"Very well," she agreed, sounding delighted by the prospect.

"I meant it when I wrote you from Brazil that we will entertain no guests at Tamar," he said, with more exasperation than veracity.

"Yes, Garth," she said obediently.

Dammit, this was not the way she was supposed to react. He had expected the threat to bring outrage, re-criminations, tears—anything but meek compliance. He felt as though he had somehow blundered into quick-sand. What the devil was he to do now?

They walked in silence through the plantation of elms and oaks and beech. As they emerged from it, they came face-to-face with Thorley, who inquired what they had been doing.

Garth replied sharply, "Getting reacquainted."

Thorley looked at him speculatively. "I trust that was enlightening."

Too enlightening for her, Sally thought uneasily. She was feeling far more compassion for Garth than she would have thought possible a few hours ago. From what little she had learned about Serena, she suspected that he was quite right when he thought they would not suit. Sally could not fault him for wanting to escape such a match.

Garth, clearly furious with her, said, "She tells me that she wishes to marry me only for my wealth."

Thorley, eager to exploit Garth's anger, said cheer-fully, "Yes, she is such an excessively extravagant chit." His face assumed an expression of deep concern. "I cannot help but wonder whether even your enormous fortune will be sufficient to keep her. Frankly, Garth, I would not blame you if you decided to end such an expensive alliance."

Garth said coldly, "Surely you know me well enough to be assured that I would never do that. Furthermore, it will not be as expensive as you seem to think." He gave Sally a look of raw challenge. "I promise you, Serena, that I shall keep you on a very small allowance, and you shall not wheedle a ha'pence more out of me. Perhaps, in light of that, it is you who will wish to cry off.''

She smiled sweetly. "Never."

His eyes narrowed angrily. "We'll see," he said, turning to leave.

Thorley asked, "What time do you expect us at Tamar today?"

"Four," Garth tossed over his shoulder. "I keep country hours."

When he was out of earshot, Thorley said exuberantly, "He is livid."

Sally knew that she should share the earl's delight, but guilt, not glee, beset her.

Emma was coming toward them, accompanied by a little boy carrying a red ball.

"That is my son, David," Thorley said proudly.

Not that he needed to tell Sally. The boy was a miniature of the earl, with the same dark hair, eyes, and coloring as his father.

David ran up to them. Sally flashed him a friendly smile, but instead of returning it, he gave her a hostile look. Then he ignored her in favor of his father.

"Greet your aunt, David," the earl prompted.

" 'Lo," he said flatly, without looking up at Sally. "Papa, will you play ball with me? P'ease, Papa." He looked at his sire with such entreaty in his big brown eyes that Thorley acquiesced.

Sally and Emma continued down the path toward the house.

"David is the image of his father," Sally observed.

"Yes," Emma agreed, "he is clearly a Keith. They all, except for Serena who is so fair, look like that."

The two women stepped through the gate into the rose arbor.

Emma asked, "How did it go with Garth?"

"He does not want to marry Serena. He believes that he and she are ill-suited."

"So they are—exceedingly ill-suited! I like Garth

very much, and it would be he who would suffer most in that union.'' Emma paused to inspect a yellow rose in full and perfect bloom. "Serena is dreadfully spoiled. Her mama cosseted her shamefully. You see, Serena was so frail when she was born that she was not expected to survive. When she did, Lady Wycombe, who could have no more children, regarded the most trifling ailments as life-threatening to Serena. The poor woman worried ceaselessly that a draught or an epidemic cold might carry her daughter off.''

Emma straightened and resumed walking along the path between the roses. "Serena became convinced she was as delicate as her mama thought her and avoided all exertion.''

Worse, Emma explained, Serena learned to exploit her mother's fears for her own ends. If she did not wish to be bothered with her lessons or some irksome social duty, she had only to plead that she was feeling poorly, and she was immediately excused. The effect upon the daughter of her well-meaning but misguided parent's indulgence was predictable. She grew up indolent in both mind and body.

Sally asked, "What of Serena's father?''

Emma frowned, her soft doelike eyes troubled. "It was odd. He adored his wife and Thorley, but he was indifferent to Serena. It is terrible to say but he did not seem to even like her. Serena pretended not to care, but she did.''

Of course she did, Sally thought. Any child would. She knew how much her own father's indifference toward his children had hurt them. But in his case, his disinterest had applied equally to all his children. Indeed, Sally sometimes doubted that her father was capable of truly loving anyone but himself.

"Yet I must give Lord Wycombe his due,'' Emma said. "He was exceedingly generous to Serena during her debut season in London. He raised no objections to all those hideously expensive clothes she ordered even though he was dreadfully under the hatches.''

Sally remembered what Thorley had said to her when he thought she was his sister: *"Why have you become so disobliging and sullen and spiteful toward your own family? What happened that day between you and Papa to turn you against us?"*

"I collect there was a quarrel between Serena and her father that drastically altered her."

Emma shuddered and the color receded from her face. "I cannot talk about it. Please, please do not ask me about it."

She broke away from Sally and hurried ahead into the house.

8

When Garth left Wycombe Abbey, he embarked upon a long, hard gallop, trying to work out some of his anger and frustration toward his betrothed before he returned home.

How the devil was he to be rid of that greedy baggage without looking like a cad? He had no intention of shackling himself to a woman who wanted him only for his fortune.

Garth felt trapped by her and by the role in life that he must now play as master of Tamar. He had never liked the estate. To him it was not a home, but an ostentatious monument to his sire's pretension and self-aggrandizement. His father had poured vast amounts of money into the house but had no interest in Tamar's lands except for the profit they could bring him. The autocratic Sir Malcolm had ridiculed all his son's suggestions to improve the estate, not because they were without merit but because they were Garth's ideas, and he had long ago lost any interest in Tamar.

Nor could a man like himself, who yearned for challenges, accept with anything but distaste the idle, useless life of an aristocratic landowner who did nothing but collect the fruits of others' labors.

Since the day Garth had sailed from Brazil for England, he had been filled with despair for the boring life, shared with an even more boring wife, that

stretched endlessly ahead of him. His spirits had not
been lifted since his return by hours spent buried in the
tedium of ledgers and numbers presented by his father's
agents who boasted to him of wringing every groat they
could out of the land.

Garth had not wanted to abandon his diplomatic career, which had given him a sense of accomplishment,
but he had promised his father that he would do so upon
Sir Malcolm's death. Honor required that he keep his
word to his late sire, just as it required that he marry
Serena.

He had gone to Wycombe Abbey that morning dread-
ing the prospect of spending a boring hour or so with
her. He could not help smiling a little ruefully, his ready
humor that he was never able to suppress for long reas-
serting itself. His visit with her certainly had not been
that. Disconcerting, baffling, infuriating, but not boring.

She was far more astute than he had suspected. Indeed, initially, he had enjoyed her company so, the
prospect of wedding her had for a moment seemed less
bleak to him, almost enjoyable. This softening ended
abruptly, however, when he learned his fortune was her
only interest. At least she had been honest with him.
He supposed he should be thankful for that.

When Garth reached Tamar, he was met by an irate
Rowena with word that Lord Eldwin Drake had disappeared.

Garth suspected that his lordship had again fled the
house to escape his sister. She gave his poor friend no
peace, dogging his footsteps like a devoted spaniel.
Garth's thoughts had been in such turmoil over Serena
that he had forgotten Eldwin and now he was assailed
by guilt for having left him so long alone at Rowena's
mercy.

"Perhaps he has gone riding as he did yesterday."

Rowena scowled. "No, he has not! I checked the
stables. He did not take a mount and his curricle is still

there. Neither his groom nor his valet has any notion where he could be.''

"Perhaps he is exploring Tamar on foot."

"No one saw him leave the house." Rowena's tone turned petulant. "I expressly told him that I would give him a tour of the grounds whenever he wished to see them. It is most rude of him if he did not avail himself of my kind offer."

"Perhaps he did not want to bother you," Garth said tactfully.

"It is all your dreadful cook's fault. Sir Eldwin vanished while I was dealing with him."

"What?" he demanded in alarm. After his return from Brazil, Garth, who had abhorred the wretched food that had been served at Tamar when his father ruled, had pensioned off the old cook. By dint of an outrageous salary and a promise of complete autonomy in the culinary realm, he had managed to lure into its kitchen a much sought after, highly temperamental French chef.

Before leaving for Wycombe Abbey that morning, Garth had approved a simple menu by English standards for that night's dinner, secure in the knowledge that while the dishes were few, Pierre would execute them to perfection.

"The menu that foreign ignoramus proposed to serve was not nearly grand enough for an earl—only four courses with two removes," Rowena said indignantly. "I daresay you have lived abroad on bachelor's fare for so long that you have forgotten what a proper English meal is."

Garth wished he could forget—quantity instead of quality! He longed to wring Rowena's short, fat neck. "I hope to God Pierre has not quit—"

"No, he has not!" she interrupted. "He tried to give notice but I informed him that he was *dismissed* without a character."

"Oh, God," Garth groaned, hurrying off to try to

soothe his prized chef's lacerated sensibilities and to persuade him to remain in his employ.

This proved to be a difficult, time-consuming undertaking—and expensive. It took Garth's promise of a handsome increase in Pierre's already huge salary and his solemn oath that *la femme lunatique* would not be permitted in the cook's august presence again.

By then, Garth had scarcely time to dress for dinner before his guests would arrive. As he emerged from the kitchen to do so, he discovered Lord Eldwin weaving unsteadily up the backstairs from the cellar.

Garth, much shocked, exclaimed, "Good God, are you bosky already?"

His lordship nodded. "I am. Don't mind telling you, my friend, you keep a fine wine cellar." He spoke with the exaggerated precision of a man who knows he is foxed and is trying to compensate for it.

"What were you doing in my wine cellar?"

"Hiding from your sister."

Garth grinned. "I always knew that Rowena could drive a man to drink."

"That woman has the instincts of a bloodhound."

"Knowing her, I'm surprised she didn't find you, even hiding as you were."

Eldwin smiled smugly. "She came down, but I hid behind a cask, and she did not see me. Don't mind telling you it is a devilishly boring way to spend the afternoon. Never cared for solitary tippling, but there was nothing to do but sample your wines."

"Sample! From the looks of you, you drank my cellar dry," Garth teased.

"Not *that* jug-bitten," his lordship protested with wobbly dignity.

Garth took his unsteady friend's arm and helped him up the stairs.

"Was the Lady Serena about today?" Eldwin asked.

"Yes." Garth longed to pour out his unhappiness and his confusion over Serena to his friend. Even if Eldwin had been sober enough to hear it, however,

Garth had never been able to discuss his deeply held emotions with anyone else.

His lordship bumped against the wall of the staircase. "Did I tell you 'bout the strolling player in Aveton yesterday who looked like Serena?"

Eldwin swayed backward and might have fallen had his host not tightened his grip on him.

Garth had seen no performer who resembled Serena with the troupe, and he dismissed his guest's claim as inebriated exaggeration. He thought again of the actress who had played Cleopatra. Even though he had told himself sternly that such a connection was beneath him, he rather regretted not having sought out the little wasp after the play.

When they reached Lord Eldwin's bedchamber, Garth turned him over to his valet to perform the daunting task of making his master sober and presentable for dinner.

Sally rejected the dress that Serena's abigail laid out for her to wear to dinner at Tamar. Beautiful as the white muslin gown was, decorated with row after row of pink ruching around the sleeves, bodice, and skirt, Sally knew without trying it on that it would not flatter her. The effect of all that horizontal decoration on a figure as petite as hers would be disastrous. She would look like a plump ball of pink and white fluff.

When Sally expressed the desire to choose for herself the gown she would wear that night, Jane led her into the huge closet where her mistress's clothes were kept, stored by type. One section jammed with silks and satins contained only dinner gowns, the next evening gowns, and a third full evening gowns. There were also, segregated into their own special sections, gowns for the theater, the opera, and court appearances, as well as carriage, promenade, morning, walking, and riding dresses.

Never had Sally seen such beautiful gowns. The stage

costumes that had previously seemed elegant to her were shabby and threadbare by comparison.

Sally was so overwhelmed that she blurted in amazement, "There's enough here to bloody well clothe an entire village."

"Aye, but milady complained frequently that she had nothing to wear, especially after the old earl died," Jane said sourly. "When the young earl discovered how deep in the River Tick his papa had left him, he told her he could afford no more of her extravagances and she would have to make do with the wardrobe she had. What a flame that put her in!"

Poor Thorley. No wonder Emma had complained that her sister-in-law was spoiled.

Sally first chose a pale blue lutestring round gown of simple construction to wear that night.

"But 'tis a *carriage* dress," the maid exclaimed, scandalized. "You cannot wear that to *dinner*."

The ever-practical Sally could not see why it mattered so long as she liked the gown, but she obediently turned her attention to the section that contained dinner dresses. Clearly there was a good deal that she did not understand about being a lady. She had not even known there were special clothes for so many different occasions, and she asked how many times a day Serena changed.

"Seven or eight," Jane answered.

Sally did not even own that many dresses. "Your mistress must spend half her life changing clothes."

"Nine-tenths," muttered the abigail tartly.

How boring to spend so much time on one's toilet, Sally thought. Perhaps the life of a lady of quality was not quite as wonderful as it appeared from a distance.

"Milady was never quite satisfied with her appearance." Jane said with a sigh.

A closer inspection of the closet's contents showed Sally why that might have been the case. Serena clearly preferred gowns heavily ornamented with ruffles, ruching, beading, floss, and other decorative clutter that would be most unflattering to a girl as tiny as she was. Worse, three-quarters of the gowns were white. It might be all the crack, but it was the one color that was guaranteed not to flatter her. Instead of looking delicate, her complexion would merely appear washed-out.

Sally finally chose the simplest dinner gown she could find. It was a rose sarcenet that did not look all that much different in style from the blue lutestring she had picked earlier. It was, however, apparently acceptable to wear that night because it resided in the section designated dinner gowns instead of the one labeled carriage dresses.

When Sally was fastened into it, she was a little shocked at how much of her bosom the gown's deep square neck revealed. Still, its color accentuated the alabaster fineness of her skin.

She wondered wistfully whether Garth would like it on her, then told herself irritably that she should not care what he thought.

But she did.

During the ride to Tamar, Sally gave Thorley and Emma a detailed account of what had transpired between her and Garth that morning.

The earl warned that the next time Garth gave her a choice between walking and riding, she should choose the latter. "Serena is far too lazy to walk anywhere."

"But I dared not because I do not know how to ride sidesaddle," Sally confessed.

"You cannot ride?" Thorley exclaimed in a tone that implied he would have been less shocked had she said she did not know how to walk.

"Oh, I can ride astride—and bareback, too."

"Astride? Bareback?" Emma echoed, appalled.

Sally explained that her father had once operated a small theater in Harrogate. In a desperate attempt to lure more patrons to this failing enterprise, he had hit upon the idea of an equestrian show, similar to the one at Astley's Amphitheater in London. The cheapest riders that he could acquire were his own children. So Sally, her older brother, and two sisters were trained in trick riding.

A wave of sadness washed over her at the memory of those days, and she fell silent. Both her brother and one of her sisters were dead now. He had succumbed three years ago of the ague and she a year later to an inflammation of the lungs.

It was Sally's opinion that the two deaths had contributed to the decline in their mother's health. For days after they had buried her sister, Mama had sat in her chair, staring blankly at the wall and muttering that perhaps it was God's punishment upon her and Papa.

When Sally had asked what could merit such terrible punishment, her father had turned upon her in a rage, ordering her never to mention the subject in front of him or her mother again. That was always her father's way of dealing with a subject he did not want to confront.

The carriage bounced as a wheel hit a hole, recalling Sally to the present. She said briskly, "I will have to write Mama in Harrogate to tell her where I am so that she will not worry."

She could not tell her mother the truth about what she was doing at Wycombe Abbey. Poor Mama would be shocked.

"I will frank the letter for you," Thorley offered. "Are you originally from Yorkshire?"

"Yes, I was born in the North Riding."

"My grandparents had an estate there," he said. "We lived on it for a time when I was small, but I was too young to remember much about it."

The carriage passed a hedgerow of hawthorn, privet, and spindle. Thorley told her that it marked the boundary between his acreage and Tamar. Sally observed that Garth's fields and orchards bore the neglected look of a landlord who squeezed everything he could from his properties and returned nothing.

When she commented on this, Emma said, "Wy-

THE FAIR IMPOSTOR   81

combe Abbey did not look much better until Thorley
inherited it. He has worked so hard to restore it.''

And now they were in danger of losing it all because
of Serena. They deserved her help, Sally thought, and
that made her feel a little less guilty about deceiving
Garth.

As they rode on, she noted in disgust how his tenants
lived in mud hovels, hardly fit for human habitation.
Her indignation grew when the carriage topped a rise
and she saw stretched out below her the massive Geor-
gian palace with majestic carved pediment and Corinthian pilasters that was Tamar.

Sally judged its creamy stone facade to be more than
two hundred feet across. On each side of the central
block, wings projected to the back. The approach was
through a formal garden, in which the plantings had
been laid out in precise circles, triangles, and ovals.

She was outraged that an owner should enjoy such
luxury while his people lived in appalling conditions.
The charity she had begun to feel toward Garth shrank.
For all his charm, he was another lazy swell reaping
the rich rewards of others' backbreaking labor and giving back nothing.

She told the Wycombes, "Sir Garth is clearly one of
those rich aristocrats who think common folk live only
for his own comfort and convenience.''

"Can't lay blame at his door,'' the earl said. "He's
only just come into control of the estate. His father, Sir
Malcolm, never spent a shilling he didn't have to unless
it was to raise his own consequence. He poured a
shocking amount of blunt into the house because he did
not think it grand enough for him.''

As their carriage approached the portico, Thorley remarked, "I daresay we shall have to endure the company of Garth's insufferable half-sister, Rowena.''

"She is one of the few things you and your sister
agree on,'' Emma said. "Serena pretended to be ill
whenever Rowena called upon her so that she would
not have to see her.''

"I cannot abide the woman," Thorley said glumly, then brightened a little. "But it will be good to see Lord Eldwin Drake again."

"Lord Eldwin will be there!" Sally exclaimed in dismay. "Oh, no!"

"Surely, you do not know him!" Thorley said. "How could you?"

Sally explained about her earlier meeting with his lordship and how she had had to convince him that she was not Serena.

"I dare not let him see me! He is certain to recognize me."

"It is too late for us to turn back; they have already seen us," Thorley said grimly, nodding toward the entrance. The double doors had opened, and two footmen had come out to help them from the carriage.

"This time around, you will have to convince Eldwin that you *are* Serena."

9

Sally dreaded meeting Lord Eldwin again. She felt as though it was opening night in a new role for which she had no time to rehearse.

As she entered the drawing room, she did what she always did when she faced a hostile audience for the first time. She took a deep, relaxing breath, and drew herself up proud and confident so that no one would suspect when she stepped on stage that inwardly she was quaking like jelly. The first lesson she had learned in the theater was that she must control her audience or it would control her.

The drawing room, however, nearly proved her undoing. She had never been in a room quite like it before. Its dimensions were larger than Papa's theater in Harrogate had been. The coved ceiling, decorated with murals of frolicking cherubs and garlands of plaster fruit, was at least thirty feet above the floor, making her feel even smaller than she was.

Never had Sally seen a less inviting room. Gilt was everywhere: on the ceiling medallion, the frieze, the intricately designed plasterwork of the walls, and the ornately carved arms and bases of the straight-back velvet settees and chairs that were lined up with military precision about the room. They looked about as comfortable to sit on as bayonets.

If this was the way rich swells liked to live, they were welcome to it.

Sally looked around for Lord Eldwin, but the only gentleman in the room was Garth, standing near the white marble fireplace midway down the enormous room. Her heart gave a little leap at the sight of him. He cut such an impressive figure in his perfectly fitted blue tailcoat and slim black pantaloons.

There was no welcome in his hard green eyes when he looked at her, and she knew that he was still angry. Not that she blamed him. A man ought to be offended by a woman who professed to want him only for his fortune.

Rowena bustled forward. "Oh, my dear, dear Lord and Lady Wycombe, how pleased and honored I am to welcome you to Tamar."

She turned to Sally, enveloping her in an embrace and an overpowering odor of violet. Rowena must have dumped the whole bloody bottle of scent on herself, Sally thought in revulsion, trying unsuccessfully to escape her grip.

"I cannot tell you how relieved I am to see you, my dearest sister," Rowena gushed. "I have been so alarmed since I learned of your illness."

She pulled back a little, and Sally paled at her breath. Stinking wortweed smelled better.

Rowena babbled, "I have not been able to rest easy until this very moment when I have seen with my own eyes, my dearest sister, that you are indeed recovered."

Sally noted that Rowena shared Serena's fondness for excessive decoration on her clothes. Although Garth's sister was several inches taller than his betrothed, she was also fat, and the tier after tier of lace flounces on her black silk gown were no more flattering to her than they would have been to Sally.

Garth came up to greet his guests. "That color becomes you," he told Sally, so coolly that she could draw no pleasure from his compliment.

Lord Eldwin, looking wobbly and unwell, tried to

slip into the room unnoticed, but Rowena rushed up to him. "Dear, dear Lord Eldwin, where have you been, you naughty, naughty boy?"

He visibly blanched, but whether at Rowena's breath or at being branded a naughty, naughty boy, Sally could not tell.

He brushed past Garth's sister with a look of loathing, but he greeted the earl and his wife with genuine enthusiasm. "Good to see you again, Wycombe, and you, too, milady."

Rowena said, "You remember my dear, dear sister, Lady Serena."

"Not your sister yet," his lordship muttered.

Sally smiled demurely up at him through her lashes, praying that he would not recognize her as an impostor.

He greeted her without suspicion. Sally, recognizing at once that he was in his altitudes, could have clapped her hands in glee and relief. Nevertheless, she slipped away from him as soon as she could and went to the other side of the room.

Thorley joined her there a minute later. "I've never known Eldwin to be a lushington before," he said. "Oh, bother, here he comes."

Weaving slightly, his lordship was making his way across the room toward Sally and Thorley.

"Lady Serena," Lord Eldwin said, slurring the name slightly, "I saw a woman yesterday who looked enough like you to be your twin. She was an actress with a group of strolling players, and—"

Sally, desperate to shut him up and change the subject before Garth or Rowena overheard him, exclaimed in outraged accents, "Surely, not a common strolling actress. How very vulgar! You insult me, Lord Eldwin."

Thorley took his cue from Sally. "Yes, by damn, you do insult my sister," he blustered with feigned indignation. "She is a lady, and jug-bitten or not, you have no right to say such contemptible things about her. You will treat her with the proper respect or answer to me."

His lordship blinked in bewilderment at the wrath that had inexplicably descended upon his head. ''Not so foxed—''

The earl ruthlessly interrupted him. ''I assure you, Eldwin, that no sister of mine would look like a strolling player, and I am shocked that you would say so.''

''Not my fault the chit looks like her,'' Eldwin said defensively. ''Don't talk like her, though.''

When dinner was announced, Garth gave his arm to Emma, the ranking lady, as he watched his betrothed out of the corner of his eye. Although he was still irate at her, he could not help but grudgingly admire her.

Few people could stand out against the dreadful excesses of Tamar's drawing room, but she did. Not only was she a beauty, but she now possessed a poise and presence that she had not two years ago.

His gaze traveled appreciatively down the rose sarcenet gown that clung to her lovely body. She even dressed more becomingly now although he could not determine why that was so. Indeed, he was rather puzzled that a gown as simply cut and lacking in decoration as hers should look so elegant on her.

Yes, Garth had to admit reluctantly that he was impressed by his betrothed, despite his ire at her reason for wanting to marry him. He was struck by the thought, as unwelcome as it was unbidden, that she would make him a wife to be proud of. Damn her greedy little heart!

At the doorway to the dining room, Garth checked for an instant, staggered by the most embarrassingly pretentious array of silver, crystal, and gold plate that he had ever seen laid out on the table and sideboard. Half a dozen wine goblets of varying shapes resided at each place. So did a bewildering assortment of spoons, forks, and knives. Every serving dish Tamar possessed must be out.

Obviously, Garth thought bitterly, Rowena had not thought the dining room grand enough for an earl.

As he guided Emma to her chair, he cast a fulminating look at his sister. She was smugly surveying her handiwork, clearly well pleased with herself and the table she had set.

Garth, who understood how his sister's mind worked, knew that she was thinking proudly that the Wycombes, who could not hope to match the display of silver and gold plates before them, must be consumed by envy.

Glancing toward his betrothed, Garth saw that she looked stunned by the ridiculous excess laid out before her—and well she might. Most likely, she had never seen anything like it before.

He was right on that point. Sally never had. She was dumbfounded at the outrageous number of dishes and utensils that the quality seemed to think necessary for their table. Having no notion what the devil she was supposed to do with all those silly implements, some of them oddly fashioned, she was terrified that her ignorance would betray her charade.

Sally was seated at Garth's left with Emma opposite her. Thorley and Eldwin flanked Rowena at the other end of the table.

Sally looked around the dining room curiously. It was as large and ornate as the drawing room had been, and she liked it no better. More murals of cherubs frolicking among cascading fruit filled the coved ceiling. More gilt decorated the walls, frieze, and ceiling. The massive straight-back chairs with their carved bases were as uncomfortable as they were ugly.

The long mahogany dining table had been shortened to a more intimate size for tonight's small party. Four dozen extra chairs were lined up along the walls with the same military precision as the settees in the drawing room.

Sally hoped that the food would be simpler than its setting or she feared that she was in for a wretched case of indigestion. If only part of what had been spent in overdecorating Tamar's dining and drawing rooms had been applied to house its tenants, they would be living in handsome cottages instead of hovels.

Glancing toward the other end of the table, Sally saw Rowena lean over to talk to Lord Eldwin. The poor man reeled back in his chair, looking green around the gills.

Must have caught a whiff of her breath, Sally thought sympathetically.

His lordship hastily reached for his newly filled wineglass and drained it. Instantly, the attentive footman in charge of the bottle quickly and unobtrusively refilled it.

Now that Sally was seated, the assortment of cutlery before her looked even more awesome than it had at a distance.

When the first course, a lobster bisque, was served, she carefully observed which of the many spoons Emma and Garth chose and followed suit.

Relieved to have passed her first hurdle without disaster, she discovered that the bisque was delicious.

Unfortunately, even though the footman who had served the soup had filled his master's bowl, he had allotted her only a few niggardly spoonfuls, not nearly enough to sustain her. She waited hopefully for him to refill her bowl, but he did not.

Finally she politely asked for more bisque.

Garth signaled immediately to a footman, but her request elicited a shocked gasp from Rowena. Clearly Sally had committed a gaffe, but she could not imagine what it had been. She inquired in a coldly polite tone, "What, pray tell, has offended you?"

"Dear, dear Lady Serena," Garth's sister said in an odiously supercilious tone, "not offended, only surprised that you should ask for more soup when it is not etiquette to do so."

More of the quality's bloody silly notions, Sally thought contemptuously. They could afford them! They never had to worry about going hungry.

Furthermore, the footman should not have been so

stingy when he ladled out her portion. Sally said with all the hauteur she could command, ''I should not have had to ask if I had been served more than three spoonfuls.''

Her reply seemed to shock Rowena even more. ''But my dearest sister, everyone knows we ladies have such delicate appetites.''

Lord Eldwin, who had been keeping the footman with the wine busy, cast a meaningful look at her ample girth and dissolved into raucous, tipsy laughter.

Rowena, oblivious to the reason for his hilarity, looked at him as though he was suddenly touched in the upper works.

Garth whispered to one of the servants. As Sally ate her replenished soup, she noticed that Lord Eldwin's empty glass had become invisible to the attentive footman with the wine bottle.

The fish course that followed the soup included both salmon and turbot. Sally watched Garth choose an odd-shaped fork and knife. Observing him, she realized that without practice in using them, they would defy deft manipulation. She left the fish untouched.

Garth attributed her abstinence to his sister's chastisement of her. Much as he might want to wring his betrothed's greedy little neck, he was embarrassed by his sister's conduct. He cold not blame Serena for wanting more of the excellent soup in light of the small quantity that had been served to her. Furthermore, he admired the spirit with which she had responded to Rowena.

Nevertheless, he ruthlessly resisted his desire to apologize for his sister's rudeness. He had seen the aversion in his betrothed's eyes when Rowena had embraced her. He suspected that his sister might prove to be his most valuable weapon in his campaign to get Serena to cry off.

As the entrée of lamb cutlet *à la princesse* with removes of venison and quail was served, a deep sigh

came from down the table and Lord Eldwin slid peace-
fully under it.

"Drunk as a lord," the host observed dryly.

To distract his guests' attention from Eldwin, Garth
launched into a series of amusing tales about Brazil and
the court of Portugal in exile there. Meanwhile, his
footmen demonstrated that they were as adept at removing an unconscious guest from beneath the table as
they were at removing plates on it.

After a dessert of vanilla cream and confiture of nec-
tarines, Garth insisted that, contrary to custom, the men
accompany the women into the drawing room instead
of lingering at the table over their port.

Sally breathed a sigh of relief that the meal was over.
By carefully studying what Emma and Garth did, then
following their example, she had managed to make it
through the dinner without committing a faux pas that
could have unmasked her as an impostor.

Actually, Sally had enjoyed the meal more than she
had expected she would. Garth's tales of Dom John, the
Portuguese Regent, and his court fascinated her. So did
the strange fauna of Brazil. She wished that she could
see with her own eyes armadillos and rheas, which
Garth described as five-foot tall birds that did not fly
and looked like ostriches, except that they had three
toes on each foot instead of two.

As they left the dining room, Rowena sidled up to
Sally. "I would be doing you no kindness, my dearest
sister, if I did not tell you that the color of your gown
is shocking."

Sally had no notion of what she could be talking
about. "Shocking?"

"Surely you know that black is the only appropriate
color for you while you are still in mourning for your
dear, dear papa."

"Good heavens," interjected Emma, who had overheard this exchange, "the earl died last summer."

"But dear, dear Lady Wycombe, it is not yet quite a

full year since he was taken from us," Rowena said stiffly.

"It will be in a few days," Emma retorted.

"I own, dear Lady Wycombe, that I do not approve of such modern notions. I intend to wear deep mourning for my papa for a year, and only then shall I go into second mourning."

"You do that," Sally interjected coldly. "I shall not presume to tell *you* how you should mourn *your* papa. I believe life is to be lived, not spent in mourning what is gone."

Her response brought an approving grin to Garth's lips.

Sally sat down on one of the red velvet sofas that was no more comfortable than her chair in the dining room had been. To her dismay, Rowena immediately settled beside her.

Garth and Thorley fell into a discussion of the Peninsular War that Sally would like to have listened to, but Rowena insisted upon telling her about the "pathetic company of strolling players" that she and her brother had watched the previous day.

"They actually had the audacity to perform *Antony and Cleopatra,*" Rowena said with a contemptuous smirk. "I wish you could have been with us, my dearest sister. I am persuaded that you would have been so amused."

Sally was not amused, but Rowena did not notice.

"And the creature who played Cleopatra," she continued, "was the most vulgar female imaginable."

Clearly, Garth's sister had been so prejudiced against Sally that no matter how fine her performance had been it would never have won her approval. That made Sally so angry that she could no longer sit beside the overbearing creature. She jumped up and went over to a marble-topped table, pretending to examine a lidded Meissen vase decorated with fanciful birds of brilliant plumage.

Behind her, Rowena's strident voice asked, "Brother,

dear, have you and dearest Lady Serena set your wedding date?''

"No," Garth answered curtly.

"My dear brother, it is long past time that you did so. Now that Serena is well again, I presume both of you are most anxious to wed.''

"You presume too much," Garth muttered.

"There is no hurry," Thorley chimed in hastily.

"Nonsense!" Rowena snapped. "They have been betrothed for years. The date should be set now so that we can begin making preparations. I own I am surprised, dear Lord Wycombe, that you take so little interest in your sister's welfare. She should have been married two years ago. She would have been had my foolish brother not had one of his queer starts about her having a come-out.''

"Thank you, dear sister," Garth interjected sardonically.

Rowena, ignoring him, turned to Sally. "I am certain that my dearest sister would like nothing better than to set the date.''

Sally would have liked nothing better than to strangle Rowena. "To the contrary, I do not feel I am quite ready for marriage yet.''

"Thank God," Garth mumbled.

"Dearest Lady Serena, I understand perfectly your hesitancy," Rowena assured Sally in her most unctuous tone. "You are very young to be mistress of such a grand establishment as Tamar. It is only natural that you should feel overwhelmed by the prospect, but you need have no fear. I have concluded that it is my duty to make my home with you so that I can guide you through the difficulties and pitfalls of running Tamar. You may happily defer to my wiser judgment, and count yourself lucky that you will have the benefit of my superior wisdom.''

In her most commanding voice—the one that brought unruly audiences to instant attention—a seething Sally said witheringly, "I neither need nor want your advice.

How dare you, *Miss* Taymor, patronize me, *Lady* Serena Keith, the daughter of the Earl of Wycombe?''

"Yes, by God," Thorley cried, jumping into the fray as he had with Lord Eldwin, "your effrontery is quite beyond the pale."

Rowena looked as though she had blundered into a hornets' nest.

Serves her right, thought Garth, who had been flabbergasted by his sister's announcement. Knowing how she thought, he had no doubt that she envisioned a brilliant future for herself in which she would be the true mistress of Tamar.

Over his dead body!

Sally said majestically, "When I am married to your brother, I—and no one else—shall be mistress of Tamar. If either you or he thinks otherwise, you are sadly mistaken."

Garth did not rise to this bait. Although he would never permit Rowena to live with him or have any say in running his home, he was quite happy to let his betrothed think he would if that would encourage her to cry off.

He should thank his sister for being so obnoxious. Rowena's determined efforts to get him and Serena to the altar might well have the opposite effect.

Garth was enjoying hugely the confrontation between the two women. To think that he had believed Serena to be a meek, colorless creature. She was magnificent when she was in a temper.

In fact, she put him forcibly in mind of that spitfire who had played Cleopatra, although why she should do so baffled him. That woman had been so dark, so different from his fair, blonde betrothed. And she had had that dreadful squint. Yet, for some reason, Serena reminded him very much of that actress.

10

Under Thorley's tutelage, Sally was completing a surreptitious lesson on riding sidesaddle in the privacy of a secluded meadow far from the curious eyes of his stable hands who would know that Lady Serena needed no such instruction.

The meadow, dotted with yellow buttercups and red spikes of common sorrel, lay along a faintly discernible path, used only by Garth as a shortcut between Wycombe Abbey and Tamar.

Sally, in Serena's indigo riding habit resplendent with gold epaulets on the shoulders and frogging on the double-breasted jacket, proved as quick a study in the saddle as she was on the stage. Thorley soon pronounced himself satisfied, but the strange saddle still felt foreign to Sally. She begged to be allowed more time to practice on it before returning to the Abbey.

Thorley pulled his gold watch from his waistcoat pocket. "I cannot stay. I am late for a meeting with my bailiff."

"You go back," Sally urged, trying to conceal how eager she was for a solitary ride, "and leave me here."

He started to protest, but Sally pleaded, "Please, this mare is so gentle that no harm can befall me."

Thorley capitulated. Sally waited until he was out of sight before nudging the mare westward toward Tamar at a lively pace. She did not enjoy the ride nearly as much as she had hoped she would because she could not balance herself on the accurst saddle as she was used to doing when she rode astride.

After a few minutes, utterly exasperated by the saddle, she left the path and reined in the mare by a copse. Gathering her billowing skirts about her, she jumped down and removed the awkward, offensive object from the animal's back.

Then she stepped into the concealing shelter of the bushes and stripped off the full skirt and several petticoats of her riding habit, revealing a pair of black breeches beneath them. Although most women would have been shocked at the thought of wearing such an unseemly garment, Sally was quite used to it. She had often played breeches' roles on the stage.

Wrapping the discarded skirts up in a bundle, she piled them and the saddle behind the trunk of an oak where they would not be visible from the path.

Then, free of the encumbrances that had prevented her from enjoying her ride, she set off at a gallop. A minute later she came upon a small pond that had been created by damming a stream to allow its waters to collect in a small depression. It looked so inviting that Sally again stopped and dismounted.

Above the pond, willows, alder, purple loosestrife, and meadowsweet grew in profusion along a rushing stream. She worked her way toward its bank through the thicket of saplings and plants that grew as high as the gold frogging on her jacket.

Sinking down beside the water's edge, Sally idly picked up a flat, gray stone and flicked it into the gurgling stream. Then she leaned back against the narrow trunk of an alder and thought of Garth. She had discovered, much to her surprise, that she liked him, and her conscience pricked her for deceiving him. Sally told herself sternly that it was too late now to have second thoughts, but that did not ease her troubled mind.

She paid no attention to the sound of a horse riding

by on the path, knowing that its rider could not see her
through the screen of willows and meadowsweet.

Only belatedly did she realize that the horse had
stopped and someone was making his way through the
undergrowth toward her.

Garth rode along the faint path that he used as a
shortcut between Tamar and Wycombe Abbey. He had
set out intent on trying once again to get Serena to
break their engagement. Yet now that he was nearing
her home, all he could think about was seeing her again.
It confounded him that he should be so eager for the
company of a maddening creature who wanted to marry
him only for his fortune.

He could not help smiling to himself at the memory
of how she had stood up to Rowena at dinner the previous night. How unfortunate that Eldwin had passed
out and missed that scene. He would have loved it.
Poor man, he had had to leave Tamar that morning,
despite his painful hangover, to attend his brother's
wedding in Cambridge. Garth would miss him, but his
friend would return to the neighborhood in three weeks
when his sister and her family took up residence at their
country home nearby.

At Garth's insistence, Rowena would also be depart-
ing Tamar today for her home in Bath, but he would
not tell his betrothed that. In his campaign to get her
to cry off, he would let her think that his infuriating
sister would make her home with them.

But did he truly want Serena to cry off?

Of course he did, he told himself firmly. He was
repelled by her reason for marrying him.

Yet he discovered in her a vitality, intelligence, and
wit that he had never suspected she possessed. She had
changed so much while he was in Brazil that it was
almost as if she were a different person.

Garth, who had always been a man who knew his
own mind, was suddenly plagued by uncertainty.

When he reached the pond where he and Thorley had

swum together as children, he was surprised to see a mare tethered near it. He would have gone on had he not noticed that the horse's saddle was missing. Alarmed that its rider might have met with some mishap, he stopped and dismounted his big bay.

Unable to find any sign of saddle or rider in the vicinity, he began following the impressions a small pair of boots had made in the tall, springy grass.

The trail led him past the pond toward the creek. As he neared the bank, he saw a flash of blue ahead of him as a woman rose to her feet. His heart gave an involuntary leap of delight as he recognized his betrothed.

Garth was more than a little astonished that Serena had ridden out to the pond alone. He would have thought her too timid to do so, but now he no longer knew what to expect from her.

Tall clumps of great willow herb concealed the lower part of her body, and he could see only her double-breasted riding coat trimmed with gold frogging and epaulets. Her matching indigo hat was decorated with two jaunty plumes. The color accentuated the whiteness of her delicate skin and the startling blue of her eyes.

His breath caught at her beauty. How fetching she looked in that high plumed hat. Once again, it struck him that a man would be proud to have such a beautiful, vibrant creature as his wife.

She stepped from behind the willow herb, and his eyes traveled down her lovely little body.

"Good God, Serena, what are you wearing!"

He required no answer to the question that had been startled out of him. It was perfectly obvious, but he still could not believe it. He had never before seen a woman, except an actress on stage, dressed in breeches.

The shocking garment was molded to her slim hips and derriere like a second skin. What it revealed stirred in him a response, as unwanted as it was intense, that suddenly played havoc with the fit of his own tight breeches.

Instead of being repulsed by her apparel, as a true

gentleman ought, he wanted nothing so much as to seize that lovely little behind and hold her to his hard body. Hastily, he half-turned away from her and stepped behind the protective cover of a purple loosestrife to hide his arousal from her. Garth did not know whether he was more disconcerted by her unladylike costume or by his response to it.

Sally was so used to wearing breeches on stage before large audiences that she was neither embarrassed nor even self-conscious in them. Yet when she saw Garth's face and how he turned away from her in apparent disgust, a sharp pain stabbed at her heart. She told herself that she ought to be delighted. After all, her goal was to repel him, and she had clearly succeeded. Yet she found no joy in his looking at her as though she had suddenly grown a head full of snakes.

Garth said sharply, "You are indecent."

"No more indecent than you are," she retorted. "You are wearing breeches, too. If they are acceptable for men to wear, why should they be indecent on a woman?"

He said through clenched teeth, "Because they are far too tight on you."

"No tighter than yours!"

He smothered a groan. Clearly, she was too innocent to realize the effect her wearing such a provocative garment would have on men. Had she ridden away from Wycombe Abbey like that? A jealous fury gripped him at the thought of the leering stable hands watching her.

"Where is your skirt?" he demanded. "Why the devil are you not wearing it?"

She told him where she had left it, explaining that it had encumbered her while she was riding.

His temper cooled when he learned that no other eyes but his own had seen her in the breeches. He said disapprovingly, "I never before thought you a hoyden."

"And you do not want to marry a hoyden?" she inquired.

"Of course not. No gentleman with any sense would." Garth firmly believed that.

So why did he feel more attracted to her now than he ever had before?

"Does that mean you are crying off?"

"No," he snapped. "Why do you look so disappointed? After all, it is *you* who wants to marry *me!* Now tell me where you left your damned skirt, and I will fetch it."

Garth turned away from her to remount his big bay. He had thought she would remain near the creek while he retrieved the skirt, but when he was in the saddle, he turned to discover that she was astride the saddleless mare. His jaw dropped in astonishment. "Surely, you do not intend to ride like that?"

A mischievous light sparkled in her eyes. "Surely, I do. I am *such* a hoyden."

They rode in silence to the copse. By the time he dismounted there, he had answered his earlier question of whether he still wanted her to cry off.

Of course he did! Her behavior this morning had proven once again what an unsuitable wife she would make him.

Yet he could not stop himself from eyeing her tantalizing derriere with longing. He was baffled by the contradictory emotions this maddening creature provoked in him.

Garth retrieved her saddle and skirt from behind the oak where she had hidden them. "What possessed you to discard these?"

Her eyes flashed challengingly. "You would not ask if you had ever ridden a sidesaddle."

"Since I have never done so," he said dryly, "I must ask."

"Sidesaddles are ridiculous contrivances that men have dictated women must use. If your sex had to use them for an hour, they would be outlawed."

"Nonsense—"

She interrupted hotly, "You say that only because you have never ridden with one. I dare you to do so."

He could not resist the challenge in those brilliant blue eyes. When he had restored the saddle to the mare's back, he swung himself confidently up. Garth hooked his legs over the two padded projections on the side of the saddle only to discover that his weight concentrated on one side of the mare made him feel alarmingly off balance.

No amount of shifting himself about in this unnatural position with only one stirrup made him feel more secure. When the mare broke into a trot, he bounced about on the seat. He could not recall in all his years of riding ever feeling more unsteady or deucedly uncomfortable.

By the time he dismounted, he was in much greater charity with his betrothed's sentiments than he was willing to admit to her. Her disdain for a sidesaddle was more sensible than he had first thought. He did not, however, want to encourage her hoydenish behavior so he fibbed, "It is not all that unpleasant."

Her eyes narrowed angrily. He was again unaccountably reminded of that squinty-eyed, black-haired actress who had played Cleopatra.

She shoved the full skirt and petticoats of her riding habit at him. "Then try it with these on, and see how hard it is."

It had been difficult enough in breeches, and he had no doubt that it would be so much worse with all those heavy skirts clinging to one's legs.

"I will take you word for it." He thrust the bundle back at her. To think he had once dismissed Serena as timid and tedious.

"What a poor-spirited creature you are!" she chided.

He grinned. "Oh, no, Sprite, you shall not provoke me into accepting your challenge. You may not scruple to make a cake of yourself in men's garments, but I have no intention of doing so in women's."

"I was merely being sensible," she insisted with frosty dignity.

Garth had to concede to himself that she had a point, although he would not admit it to her. Instead, gesturing at her skirts, he said sternly, "For God's sake, put them back on before someone else happens along and sees you."

Obediently, she disappeared behind a bush.

As he waited for her, he paced irritably back and forth, trying to sort out his seething emotions. Without the provocation of her lovely body before his eyes, he could think more rationally. Nothing could be more contrary to his image of what he wanted in a wife than a hoyden in breeches. Yet appalled as he was, he admired her spirit—and admired even more her enticing body.

One thing was certain. He had never known another woman like her.

The rustle of parting bushes drew his attention. She emerged once again dressed in her riding skirt and petticoats.

Garth immediately regretted no longer being able to see the tantalizing curves of her derriere and hips that the breeches had revealed.

He was shaken by an intense longing to capture the lovely little sprite in his arms. Staring down at her upturned face, he could not resist an overpowering urge to kiss her delectable mouth. He bent his head, intent on doing so.

Instead of yielding her lips to him, she backed hastily away.

Disappointed and more than a little miffed that she wanted to evade his kiss, he said brusquely, "Why do you draw back from me when you profess to want to marry me?"

Sally was too good an actress to let him see the battle that was warring within her. She wanted nothing more than to kiss him. Indeed, she had never before wanted to kiss a man so much, but she instinctively feared that if she did, she would be lost.

Feigning indignation to cover her own confused emotions, she demanded, "And why would you want to kiss me if you do not want to marry me?"

Her question startled him into retorting, with more honesty than wisdom, "Men frequently kiss girls they do not want to wed."

"I see," she said coldly. "You are a rakehell then."

Much nettled, he snapped, "No, I am not." Good God, her tongue was as shocking as her apparel! "That is not a word that should disgrace a lady's lips."

"It seems to me it is the man she describes who is the disgrace. Why should a woman be barred from speaking the truth simply because it is unpleasant?"

Again, Garth could not argue with her logic.

Nor could he understand how he could simultaneously be so attracted and provoked by a woman.

11

Garth returned to Tamar, wishing that Lord Eldwin had not already departed. He desperately wanted to confide his confusion over Serena, but then he realized that even if his friend had still been there, he most likely would not have done so. Garth was not a man who gave his confidences easily. Always he had kept his emotions, his aspirations, his frustrations, even his conflicts with his father bottled up deep within himself, unable to discuss them with anyone.

He spent much of the next twenty-four hours trying to deal with his contradictory emotions toward his betrothed.

By reminding himself repeatedly of what he required in a spouse, he finally succeeded in overcoming with cold logic the heat of his desire for her. She would not do as his wife, and he resolved to convince her of this before another day passed.

Considering how best to do so, he hit upon taking her to the cascade. It was his favorite place at Tamar, but when he had brought Serena there two years ago, she had hated it. To him, their diametrically opposite reactions to this lovely spot epitomized how incompatible they were.

When he went to Wycombe Abbey to request that she go for a ride in his curricle with him, he did not tell her their destination, saying it was a surprise.

103

They set out at a brisk pace through Tamar's park. When they stopped beside the path that led to the cascade, he helped her from his equipage.

They strolled through a wood of oak mixed with wild cherry and crab apple. When they emerged from it, the terrain grew more hilly, with clumps of mock orange and wild rhododendron crowding the path. The day was exceptionally fine: warm and sunny, with only a few white clouds billowing on the western horizon.

Ahead of them, a creek with yellow iris and great willow herb along it burbled down a hillside and plunged over a rock slab as high as a man's shoulder, creating a miniature waterfall.

"Oh, how—" his betrothed exclaimed, then hastily clapped her hand over her mouth. Her look of delight gave way to acute discomfort.

Garth was puzzled by her odd reaction. Serena had been here a number of times, yet for an instant she had looked as though she had never seen it before. "What is it about the waterfall that startled you?" he asked.

"Nothing, nothing. It was not that. I—er, remembered something that I forgot." She put her hands to her flushed cheeks as though to cool them.

They sat down upon a wooden bench that had been strategically placed near the base of the cascade so that its occupants could watch the waterfall.

Garth cast a sidelong gaze at his companion. Contrary to his last encounter with her, when she had been wearing those shocking breeches, she presented the perfect picture of a demure young lady of quality in her high-necked, unadorned gown of pink muslin.

He had to stifle another sudden urge, as powerful as it was unsettling, to kiss her. He must be going mad. After all, he was here to get her to break their engagement.

An invisible mist thrown up by the tumbling water floated on the light breeze, enveloping them in refreshing coolness.

She tilted her chin so that her face could better catch

it. "How good the spray feels," she murmured happily.

Garth's jaw dropped in surprise. When he had brought Serena here two yeas ago, she had complained vehemently that the transparent mist ruined her hair and gown.

Nor, she had grumbled then, could she understand why anyone would want to walk so far for the privilege of being soaked. Between that and a scarcely discernable breeze that Serena had stigmatized as a dreadful wind, she had wailed that she was certain to contract a fatal inflammation of the lungs.

Serena's overconcern with her health, which had caused her to avoid fresh air during his visit two years ago, had disgusted Garth. It had been his unflattering opinion that her frailty was more imagined than real and that she used it to manipulate her anxious relatives into doing her bidding.

In one of his letters to her from Brazil, written with the sole intent of getting her to cry off, he had maliciously advised her to bathe in an icy creek to harden her constitution.

Now, she observed, "Such a romantic spot." She turned to him, her blue eyes sparkling mischievously. "Is that why you brought me here?"

Nothing had been further from his mind. He had intended to use it as a persuasive setting for getting her to end their engagement, but now the aggravating minx, who had complained bitterly about the place two years ago, professed to find it romantic. In his frustration, he longed to shake her.

Instead, leaning back against the bench, he said, "It is my favorite spot at Tamar."

She looked at him with a smile so irresistible that it drove from his mind all thought of his purpose in bringing her here.

"I understand why," she said, still smiling.

"When I first saw this cascade as a small child, I thought it so grand," he said musingly, "but I fear that seeing the great Niagara Falls in America spoiled me. They plunge more than 150 feet.''

Her eyes widened in wonder. "Truly?" she asked. "Oh, tell me about them!''

He complied, and she began to ask questions about other things that he had seen in America. She seemed not to have the smallest recollection that when he had tried to tell her about that country two years ago, she had said coldly that she had no interest in hearing a single word about a land of rebels and savages.

Garth wondered if her belated interest was feigned, but he soon concluded that it was real. Her questions were not perfunctory but full of genuine curiosity. They were often astute as well. She was not the pea-goose that he had thought her.

"How exciting it must have been," she said, sounding a little envious.

"Too exciting sometimes," he said wryly, thinking of some of his more harrowing experiences in the wild interior.

When he described one of them, ending it with an amusing twist that mocked himself, he was so charmed by her laugh, light and melodious as a flute's song, that he recounted several of his more humorous misadventures in order to provoke it again.

His efforts were richly rewarded both by her laughter and the deep interest that was mirrored in her beautiful face.

Garth's descriptions of America were so vivid that Sally felt as though she could see it in her mind's eye. Some of his tales were hilarious, and, as often as not, at his own expense. She knew very few men who could laugh at themselves as he did, and his self-deprecating humor charmed her. A man as puffed up in his own consequence as she had initially thought him would never make the kind of admissions he did.

And he was sinfully handsome with those luminous green eyes, that engaging grin, and his wayward wave of golden-brown hair tumbling across his forehead. She longed to reach up and brush it back.

Apparently sensing her scrutiny, Garth gave her a smile of such brilliance that her heart somersaulted.

Her dislike of him was turning into something warmer.

Much warmer.

Suddenly Sally wanted to know everything she could about him.

"What prompted you to become a diplomat?" Emma had told her that Garth had spent nearly a decade in Vienna, Rome, the new United States of America, and Brazil. Sally could understand the attraction of Vienna or Rome, but why would a man as rich as he was subject himself to the dangers and discomforts of living in half-civilized lands like the United States or Brazil?

He said, "I love the adventure and the opportunity to see new lands." His smile faded, and he said a little bitterly, "Besides, diplomacy was the only career that my father could be persuaded to allow me, other than standing for parliament, which I had no wish to do."

"If your father had permitted it, what career would you have pursued?"

Garth hesitated, then decided to tell her the truth. It would horrify the snobbish Serena. "You will be shocked. My dream was to become an actor."

Sally suspected that this ambition, like some of his ancestors he had told her about, was a figment of his imagination—part of his campaign to get her to break their betrothal. Surely, he knew his own worth too well to have ever considered so disreputable an occupation as acting. But why had he picked that particular profession, she wondered nervously. Could it be that he suspected the truth about her?

"Has my base ambition revolted you?"

"To the contrary," she said sweetly, "I applaud it for two reasons. First, I think it most admirable for a man to pursue a craft rather than waste his life in idle leisure. Second, I do not believe that you ever had any such ambition.''

''If I did not, why would I tell you such a thing about myself?''

''For the same reason that you told me about Cut-throat Charlie and Peg-leg Pete.''

She had that right, Garth thought grumpily, much disappointed that she had not been repelled by his interest in acting. Was there *nothing* that he could do to provoke her into crying off?

God help him, she was determined to wed him.

But would marriage to her be such a bad thing?

Garth studied her intently. Fine droplets of mist glistened on her lovely little face. Again he was reminded of a wood sprite.

No longer was she the timid, colorless ninnyhammer, without spirit or wit and oblivious to every suit, that she had been two years ago. Even her beauty, in his opinion, had improved. Her eyes glowed, and he found her smiling mouth well nigh irresistible.

Garth was still angry at her for wanting to marry him for his money even though she thought him beneath her. When he reflected on it, however, he had done everything he could to give her an aversion to him. All of his letters to her from Brazil had been written with that express intent.

He wagered that were he to try, he could quickly give her much more valid reasons for wanting to wed him. The challenge excited him, and a calculating little grin tugged at his lips.

But if he set out to make her fall in love with him, he would have to marry her. Garth was still not certain that he wanted to do that. What he needed was more time with her to ascertain whether the sea change in her during the past two years was real or affected.

''I was not pitching gammon, Sprite, when I said I wanted to be an actor.''

''Then why did you not become one?''

''The answer is perfectly obvious, is it not? The heir

to a baronetcy and a great fortune does not disgrace his family by such shocking behavior. My father made my duty very plain to me.''

Something about the set of Garth's face told Sally that he was a man who took duty very seriously, and she liked him the better for it.

''Fortunately for me, my uncle—my mother's brother— was appointed ambassador to the court in Vienna the summer after I finished at Oxford and proposed to take me with him as one of his junior secretaries. I leaped at the opportunity, but it took all of my uncle's highly persuasive powers to win my father's permission. Papa agreed to it only after I swore that I would give up diplomacy upon his death and return home to England to oversee my inheritance.''

''So that is why you resigned.''

''Yes, I could not go back on my word to my father— or to anyone else.'' He smiled wryly at her. ''Whatever my other failings, I am a man of honor.''

Garth's smile faded, and he stared at the waterfall with unhappy eyes. ''My father was outraged that I wanted to accomplish something useful with my life instead of wasting it on idle pleasures.''

This admission both surprised and discomforted Sally. She had initially believed Garth was another one of those fribbles, like the pair who had accosted her in Aveton, who cared only for their own pleasures. She had had little compunction about deceiving such a man, but now that he was turning out to be so very different, she was beginning to hate herself.

Garth, his voice edged with bitterness, said, ''Papa's most fervent wish was to be an aristocrat, and the nobility does not stoop to gainful employment.''

''Ah, yes,'' Sally observed, '' 'Idleness is an appendix to nobility.' ''

Garth looked incredulous. ''That's from Robert Burton's *The Anatomy of Melancholy*, isn't it? I would not have thought such a work to your taste.''

"Well, you are wrong. I warned you that I had book-ish tendencies."

"When it comes to you," he said, an odd light in his eyes, "I seem to have been wrong about a good many things."

Sally's heart fluttered. She would have liked to ask him what things he had been wrong about, but she dared not. Instead she changed the subject abruptly, asking him whether part of the attraction of a diplomatic career had been the opportunity it afforded to escape his father.

"How perceptive of you," he exclaimed in surprise. "Although I collect it is no secret that my father and I did not get along. We were so very different."

"Would you have remained a diplomat after his death had it not been for your promise to him?"

Garth had thought that he would have, but now he was less certain. "I don't know. Although I love visit-ing foreign lands, I think that I shall be quite content to reside in England again. I missed this country more than I ever thought I would."

Garth was discovering that putting these thoughts into words helped him to clarify them.

"No," he decided aloud, "it is not living abroad that I shall miss, but my work. It gave me a raison d'être."

The sympathy and understanding Garth saw in his betrothed's eyes prompted him to confide in her as he had never before done with anyone. "But I did not miss Tamar. I have never liked it, perhaps partly because I was so unhappy here as a child, but also because the house is so cold and ostentatious—palatial splendor in-stead of comfort. I would much prefer a home that is inviting to one designed only to enhance one's conse-quence."

Glancing toward the western horizon, Garth was startled at how far toward it the sun had descended. He could not believe how quickly the time with his sprite had passed.

Hastily, he rose from the oak bench and held out his

hand to help her to her feet. "Come, we must get back before your brother sends out a search party for us."

He did not release her hand as they retraced their steps down the path between the mock orange and wild rhododendron. Nor did Sally want to withdraw it. His grasp was strong and warm and comforting. Her heart gave an odd, happy little lurch. She had never before known that holding a man's hand could be so exciting.

When they were a hundred yards from his curricle, still screened from their view by the rhododendron lining the curving path, he stopped and turned to her.

His eyes, as soft as green velvet, met her gaze and held it in silence.

Sally wondered helplessly whether Garth would try to kiss her again as he had the previous afternoon, but he moved no closer.

Instead, he slowly, gravely raised her hand to his mouth. His hypnotic eyes never wavered from hers as he brushed his lips caressingly over the back of her hand, then lingeringly along her fingertips.

Sally trembled. A peculiar yearning, unlike anything she had ever felt before, seized her.

When he silently lowered her hand and started down the path again without attempting to capture her lips, Sally ached with disappointment and a strange, gnawing frustration.

12

Sally and Emma walked in the rose arbor, stopping from time to time to examine an especially flawless bloom that had unfurled its velvety petals.

"How beautiful it is here," Sally said, breathing deeply of the sweet, rose-scented air. "I cannot understand how Lady Serena could have run away from such a beautiful spot."

"She hated it here," Emma said. "If she had her way, she would live exclusively in London. Unlike you, she has no interest in nature, only in her clothes and *ton* parties.

Sally could not fathom how Serena could possibly prefer the noise and smoke and soot of London to the peace and beauty of this idyllic spot—nor another man to Garth.

Remembering what Lord Eldwin had said about Leland Caine, Sally wondered again whether Thorley's certainty that Serena was with Netta Bridger was unwarranted.

Gathering her courage, she said to Emma, "I collect that you are not as convinced as your husband that Lady Serena is with Netta Bridger, rather than Lord Leland Caine."

The countess stopped abruptly and faced Sally. Her face was partially shaded by her straw bonnet trimmed with pink ribbons, but there was no mistaking the anxiety that creased her brow.

"No, I am not," she admitted. "Thorley believes that even Serena could not be such a goosecap as to elope with him. I hope that he may be right, but I am not so sanguine."

"Is she in love with Lord Leland?"

"More in love with his pedigree than with him, I should think," Emma said with uncharacteristic sharpness. "He is the Duke of Hardcastle's youngest child, and Serena was determined to leg-shackle a duke's son. It was all that dreadful Netta's doing. She turned Serena against Garth. Why, I don't know. When he was home two years ago, Netta seemed to like him well enough. Indeed, I strongly suspected her of having a *tendre* for him, but he could not abide her."

"I collect Lord Leland was much taken with Serena."

"Not initially. It was she who set out to fix Lee's interest. However, I am persuaded that now he is sincerely enamored with her."

"What is he like?" Sally asked. "Is he handsome?"

"Not handsome—beautiful. That is not a complimentary adjective to apply to a man, but that is what he is. His curls are as golden as yours, and he has the most melting smile. His features are perfection itself, and a woman would die to have those limpid blue eyes and thick, curling lashes."

"He sounds irresistible."

"I find him highly resistible," Emma said. "Lee's mental gifts are as inferior as his physical are superior."

The two women resumed walking toward the house.

"Not to wrap it in clean line, he is a blockhead," Emma said candidly. "Exceedingly amiable, but an appalling slowtop nonetheless. Of course, Serena's understanding is not quick either. If it were, she would see at a glance that Garth is far superior to Lee in every respect save social standing."

Sally recalled that Lord Eldwin had said much the same thing.

Emma stopped to pluck a withered red rose from a bush that they were passing. "In truth, I think Lee and Serena are well suited. They are both bird-witted and indolent. They despise exertion, and their conversation is limited to the most tiresome commonplaces. They would bore more lively mates, but they seem to find each other fascinating company."

"I collect you do not like your sister-in-law overmuch."

"I used to be quite fond of her," Emma said pensively, "but she changed so much the past year that my patience wore thin."

Thorley's plaintive questions echoed again in Sally's ears: *"Why have you become so disobliging and sullen and spiteful toward your own family? What happened that day between you and Papa to turn you against us?"*

Three days after their first visit to the cascade, Garth brought Sally there again, this time with a basket of food that his estimable Pierre had prepared for them.

Sitting on a blanket spread near the water, they ate such delicacies as *saumon au beurre, tourte parmerienne,* and *la brioche au fromage,* which Sally discovered were fancy French names for salmon with butter, chicken and pork pie, and cheesecake. The dishes by whatever name were so delicious that soon nothing was left of this portable feast except a large bunch of grapes.

Contented and a little sleepy from all the food, Sally turned her face toward the cascade. A brief gust of wind carried its spray to her, enveloping her for an instant in its cooling mist.

The air was fragrant with woodland scents. She wished that her mama could see this spot. She would love it so.

Sally smiled at Garth. "How pleasant it is. Did you come here often when you were a child?"

"No, I spent very little time at Tamar then."

The unruly wave of golden-brown hair fell across his forehead, and it was all Sally could do to smother the urge to reach up and brush it back.

"My mother avoided Tamar and my father as much as she could. She was married to him against her will, you know." Bitterness edged Garth's voice. "Her father, Lord Garth, for whom I was named, was all to pieces, and Papa was delighted to pay well for the connection to such a distinguished family."

"Your parents' union was not a happy one?"

"No," he said, brushing the wayward hair from his forehead. "Fortunately for Mama, she came from a large family and could manage to escape my father for much of the year by visiting various members of it. Happily for me, I always accompanied her."

His mother had died when Garth was thirteen, but he had been at Eton by then, so he had continued to avoid spending much time at Tamar where his remote, ambitious father ruled with an irascible temper and depressing formality.

Now, recalling those brief duty visits, he confessed that he had discovered himself so different from his clutch-fisted, social-climbing father and half-sister, who had nagged him unmercifully, that he had felt like a changeling.

Once again Garth found himself telling the sprite things he had never told another soul. How comfortable he was with her. Breaking off a small bunch of grapes, he handed it to her.

"I understood why Mama was so unhappy with Papa. That is why, having been exposed to the hell of forced wedlock, I was so averse to entering it."

"Was?" Sally blurted, startled by his use of the past tense.

His only answer to her query was an enigmatic smile. He said musingly, "I used to envy Thorley. I think your papa and mama would have done anything for each other. They seemed so happy together."

Perhaps Serena's parents had been, but Sally's had

not. She suspected that her own mother had not been much happier with her selfish, volatile husband than Garth's had been, although her parents' economic circumstances had been far bleaker.

Theirs had been the poverty-stricken lot of most provincial actors. For Mama, there had been no escape to wealthy relatives. Her parents had been so destitute the cold, brutal winter Sally was born that the whole family might have starved or frozen to death had not a kindly lady in the North Riding taken a liking to Mama. She had given shelter to Mrs. Marlowe, pregnant with Sally, and to her family. Sally had often wondered who the woman was, but neither of her parents would ever talk of their benefactress or of that winter. Indeed, nothing was more certain to touch off her father's explosive temper than to mention that time.

After that, they had gone to York and then to London where Mama, a far better thespian than her husband, might have won an enduring position on the London stage had it not been for him. Covent Garden had offered her a place, but none for Mr. Marlowe. Papa, the only person in the world who considered himself a great actor, had fulminated that the theater would either take them both or would have neither. Covent Garden still declined his services.

Despite Mama's tearful pleadings to remain in London where at least she could make a comfortable living for their family, he had insisted that they return to Yorkshire. He refused, he had thundered, to become another Sid Siddons, a mere theatrical appendix to his actress wife, the great Sarah.

So Papa, who always satisfied his own desires ahead of all else, had taken what money they had saved and, over his wife's objections, bought a small theater in Harrogate. Sally had been amazed that her parents could have managed to set aside that much money.

Unfortunately, Papa had not been much better as a theatrical manager than he had been as an actor, and the establishment slid slowly toward ruin.

Two years ago he had lost it, and her parents had been forced to join the Walcott Strolling Players.

Garth said, "Perhaps I should not have mentioned your parents. You look so sad. I collect you still grieve for them?"

"Yes," Sally answered truthfully. Although they were not dead as Garth thought, she grieved for the unhappiness of their lives, two ill-suited people bound for life.

The more Sally learned about Serena, the better she understood Garth's reluctance to marry her. They would be as unhappy together as his parents had been. Sally told her nagging conscience that she was doing both Serena and Garth a favor by trying to get him to abort a marriage that neither wanted.

Sally broke off a grape from the bunch Garth had given her. Before popping it into her mouth, she asked, "Do you dislike living at Tamar now?"

He shrugged. "Boredom rather than dislike is my major difficulty. I do not find devoting myself to increasing an already huge fortune a very exciting or—worthy—prospect."

Garth leaned back and propped himself on his elbow. He said with a lopsided little grin that tugged at Sally's heart, "You see, Sprite, I have this odd notion that I should like to leave the world a better place for having lived in it."

She admired his ambition, yet it seemed at such odds with the way his tenants lived. Candid as always, she cried, "But you are wrong! There is so much you can accomplish at Tamar. Only look around you at the abysmal state to which its lands and tenants have been reduced. You can start by replacing the hovels in which your dependents live. Improving their lot and your land would be worthy work indeed."

For a moment Garth could only stare at her. He had always been vaguely ashamed of the way that his father had exploited his estates. And secretly embarrassed as he passed those pathetic shacks that his father's workers and tenants lived in on his way to the wretched excess of Tamar. He had even argued once long ago with his father to build them better dwellings.

A stirring of interest arose in Garth. He was under no obligation to administrate the estate in the same niggardly fashion that his sire had.

Why, he could even fulfill his ambition, so ridiculed by his father, of gathering cuttings and seeds from the four corners of the earth to create an arboretum at Tamar that would rival what Sir Joseph Banks had created at Kew.

Suddenly Garth was more excited than he had been since he had boarded the ship that carried him back to England from Brazil. He had been so caught up in his unhappiness over abandoning his diplomatic career and returning home to marry a boring female and live an even more boring life, that he had failed to recognize the opportunities it offered. He could not believe he had been so blind.

All the pent-up energy that had no outlet all these weeks was suddenly focused on the challenge of transforming his properties into something he could be proud of.

His mind full of plans, he was suddenly anxious to begin implementing them. He rose from the bench and gave Sally his hand. The future no longer seemed tedious, but exciting, full of challenge—thanks to his sprite. He smiled happily at her.

As they started down the path toward his curricle, he said almost in wonder, "I believe you will make Tamar a fine mistress."

She stopped dead and turned to stare at him. For some strange reason, his compliment seemed to have dismayed her.

She asked coldly, "What of Rowena? She thinks she is its mistress."

"I would never permit Rowena to live with me. That is why I sent her back to Bath three days ago."

Her eyes narrowed. "You did not tell me that you had done so."

He felt his face redden. "It—er, slipped my mind."

"I do not like your sister," she said bluntly.

Garth sighed. "Not many people do. I confess that she frequently mortifies me. She did so only a few days ago with a company of strolling players."

A note of ice crept into his companion's voice. "Yes, she told me about that dreadful actress who played Cleopatra."

"Rowena is guilty of unadulterated slander! I have never seen a better Cleopatra. The actress gave a remarkable— Why are you looking at me so strangely, Sprite?"

His unexpected praise of Sally's performance had so surprised her that she was gaping at him.

"What is it?" Garth prodded.

When she did not answer him, he gave a rueful little toss of his head. "Poor Rowena loves nothing so much as to feel superior to those around her—perhaps because in her heart she knows that she is not. She ridiculed those strolling players before she had even seen them perform. I wanted to throttle her."

Yet Sally had heard him tell Rowena that he did not want to waste his time watching bumpkins perform. She asked coolly, "Did you tell her how unfair she was?" Sally already knew the answer, but she wanted to hear how Garth would reply.

"God, no. If I had, Rowena would have flown into the boughs and made an even greater cake of herself. I tried as unobtrusively as possible to get her to leave by telling her that we would be wasting our time to watch them. But she insisted upon staying."

Suddenly Garth's eyes glowed with what was obviously a cherished recollection. "I wish you could have been there. The actress who played Cleopatra gave Rowena the trimming that she deserved. I am persuaded you would have enjoyed it as much as I did."

Their eyes met, and the look in Garth's made Sally's heart turn over.

"Oh, my Sprite, suddenly there is so much I want to share with you!"

He smiled at her, that brilliant smile which embraced his entire face and warmed her like the sun. Sally felt as though she could not breathe. She stared longingly at him, at his slim, sharply etched face with the wave of golden-brown hair on his forehead.

God help her, she was falling in love with Garth.

To do so was madness.

She was mad!

Sally wondered helplessly, yearningly, what it would be like to be kissed by that smiling mouth.

As though he read her mind, his head dipped and his lips captured hers in a long slow kiss that started out as soft and sweet as honey, then exploded into a melding that was as hot and consuming as fire.

Sally had been kissed before, on stage and off, and she had never understood why a woman would enjoy it.

Now she understood.

Garth's kiss was as different from the others as the harsh light of day was from the velvet softness of night.

She was lost.

13

Master David Keith, having made good his escape from the nursery while his nurse was under the misapprehension that he was still napping, was trying with notable lack of success to bowl a hoop across Wycombe Abbey's south lawn when Sally came upon him.

He had clearly indulged in the novel experiment of dressing himself. The tails of his shirt hung out of rumpled corduroy breeches, its collar was askew, and its buttons had been fastened in whatever hole had been handiest.

After watching him struggle for a minute with the recalcitrant hoop, Sally said cheerfully, "Let me show you how it's done."

Normally, she had an excellent rapport with children, but all her overtures to David during her four weeks at Wycombe Abbey had been rebuffed. He either ignored her or ran away when she approached him, and he looked now as though he were about to flee.

Before he could, however, she took the hoop from his hand and showed him how to manipulate it.

In another quarter hour under her tutelage, he was bowling the hoop like an expert and enjoying himself hugely. So was she.

Suddenly, he stopped and looked up at Sally, his little face much puzzled.

"What's wrong?" she asked.

"Who is 'ou?"

"You know who I am," she answered warily. "I am your aunt."

"No, 'ou isn't," he said emphatically. " 'Ou look 'xactly like her, but 'ou isn't."

Out of the mouths of babes, Sally thought, much shaken that this toddler should have discerned the truth. "Why would you think I am not your aunt?"

" 'Ou's nice," he said succinctly. "She's not."

Startled, Sally blurted, "Why not?"

"She says I plague her, and I don't!" His underlip protruded stubbornly. "Why do 'ou pr'ten' to be her? Even my mama thinks 'ou is her."

"Yes, she does," Sally lied. It would be better that the child not know his parents were part of the deception. She had to find a way, though, to keep him from saying anything to his nurse or someone else.

"Your aunt and I have a wager that no grown-up can tell that I am not her. So far, none of them has been able to." She squeezed his hand. "Will you promise to keep my secret and not tell anyone so that I can win my wager?"

"If 'ou will play with me again," he bargained.

"Gladly," she assured him.

He grinned happily. "I promise. I wish 'ou was my aunt."

Sally hugged the little boy to her. "I wish I were, too." Then she would truly be Garth's betrothed.

David's nurse, having discovered her charge was missing from his bed, rushed out to collect him for his belated nap.

Sally, seeing Emma step onto the terrace overlooking the east lawn, joined her, sinking into a chair beside hers. Not a cloud shielded the earth from the sun, and Sally was thankful for the shade the Abbey's east front provided the terrace.

When she related to Emma what her son had said, the countess was aghast. "It never occurred to me that he would guess you were not Serena. He's so little, and she never paid any heed to him.''

''That's the problem. Not knowing that, I did,'' Sally said. ''David says that she does not like him.''

Emma's mouth thinned. ''She doesn't. I had not realized that he was so perceptive.''

''How could she possibly not like him? He is such a delightful child.''

Emma said unhappily, ''Serena did not like any of us the past year. You would have to ask her why.''

''Why have you become so disobliging and sullen and spiteful toward your own family? What happened that day between you and Papa to turn you against us?''

Emma patted her face with her white linen handkerchief. ''This dreadful heat has robbed me of my energy and my appetite. If you do not object, I shall order only a light dinner for us tonight since Thorley will not be here.''

''Where is Thor going?''

''He and Garth have been invited to dine with Lord Conroy. I count us fortunate that the dinner is for gentlemen only, and we are not invited. Conroy sets a wretched table.''

Garth had said nothing to Sally about going to Conroy's instead of calling on her, as he did every night, and she was surprised at how disappointed she was that she would not see him.

He rarely came to Wycombe Abbey during the day because he was so busy supervising his remarkable transformation of Tamar. Since that afternoon at the cascade three weeks ago, Garth had thrown himself into this project with an energy and enthusiasm that amazed her. The entire countryside was agog over all that he was doing to improve his estate and its tenants' welfare.

Already construction was starting on sturdy cottages. In his determination to improve his land and its production, he had immersed himself in *A Treatise on Practical Farming* by John Alexander Binns, a farmer from Loudon County, Virginia. Now Garth intended to experiment with crop rotation, deep plowing, the use of gypsum as fertilizer, and other innovations discussed in the book. He had also marked off several acres that he planned to transform into an arboretum, and he was busy writing letters, seeking cuttings for it.

Nor were his changes confined to his land. He closed up Tamar's overdecorated state apartments, which he confessed he had always despised, and was using another suite of rooms, redone in a comfortable, informal style, for his living quarters.

Sally had thought Garth just another slothful swell, but she had been mistaken. His restless, abundant energy had needed only to be directed into a channel that challenged him. One more example of how wrong her initial impressions of him had been.

She could scarcely believe that a person could have been simultaneously as happy and as miserable as she had these weeks at Wycombe Abbey. With each passing day, Sally liked Garth more and herself less for deceiving him.

When she had agreed to this charade, she had told herself that because neither Garth nor Serena wanted their marriage, no one would be truly hurt by the deception.

Now Sally knew that for the cruel lie it was. At least one person would be deeply hurt.

Herself.

Worse, the deception was an abject failure. Even Thorley had conceded more than a week ago that his ill-conceived plan had been a disaster.

He had conceded, too, that Sally had scrupulously complied with his instructions on how to get Garth to cry off. She had made him think that she was eager to marry him for his money. At every opportunity, she had gamely engaged him in dialogues on subjects too weighty for a woman's frail mind, hoping to convince him that she was one of those bluestockings he detested. It was clear, however, that her sudden erudition had more surprised than disgusted him.

Thorley had confessed, "I was insane to have asked you to pose as Serena, but I was so desperate I was no longer thinking clearly! I believed that it would so easy, that it would not take you more than a few days to get him to break the engagement. How wrong I was! And I did not even consider what we should do if my plan failed."

That was the problem. They could not come up with a satisfactory way out of this coil. Were they to tell Garth the truth, he would be justifiably enraged at how he had been duped. He would insist upon immediate repayment of the loans, and the Wycombes would be ruined.

In desperation, they had continued the hoax, not because they wanted to, but because they did not know what else to do.

Sally cursed herself for letting Thorley talk her into his plan. How richly she deserved Preston Walcott's oft-voiced criticism that she let her love of a challenge and adventure pitchfork her into trouble.

That night after dinner, Sally was in the library searching for a book when the door knocker sounded. A minute later, the butler appeared to inform her that Sir Garth awaited her in the drawing room.

Much surprised, she hurried to join him there.

When he saw her, his eyes gleamed approvingly. "How lovely you look tonight, my Sprite."

It was so hot that she had put on the merest wisp of a green muslin dress that she would never have worn had she thought Garth would call. Its waist was gathered so high beneath her bosom and its square neck cut so low that only a slender band of flimsy cloth lay between them. The rest of the gown was no more generously cut, and the thin muslin clung to her body. She blushed at how much it revealed of her.

The hot intensity of Garth's gaze resting on the curve of her breasts disturbed her. A rosy flush colored her pale skin, and she put her hand up as though to shield herself from his eyes.

His laugh was husky. "If you did not want me to see you in that dress, Sprite, why did you wear it?"

"Because it is so hot, and I did not expect you tonight."

"Why not? You know I come every night."

"I thought that you were dining at Lord Conroy's with Thor."

The amusement vanished from Garth's face at her mention of Conroy's name. "I declined the invitation," he said curtly. "Conroy only rusticates when he is under the hatches, and I dislike being importuned to rescue him."

"Surely he would not do so while you were his guest?"

"Yes, he would. I have known him since we were at Oxford together. He finds me worthy of his company only when his pockets are all to let."

"What a dreadful man!"

Her empathy prompted Garth to tell her how bitterly he had resented certain scions of highly titled fathers like Conroy. With pockets all to let, they had been eager to embrace him as their boom companion in return for his pulling them repeatedly from the River Tick. They were astonished that he had no taste for their company and shunned it in favor of friends who liked him for himself.

"That won me a reputation for being quite as much of a pinch-purse as my father." Although it was undeserved, as a number of friends who had benefited from his generosity could testify, Garth had encouraged it.

"Did that bother you?" she asked.

"No, it spared me the unwanted overtures of men who would be my friend for a price." Once again, Garth was amazed at how easily he could confide his long-hidden feelings to her.

Not only was she lovely, but she was vibrant and intelligent and compassionate, with a delightful sense of humor, virtues that Garth had once thought she lacked entirely.

What a puzzle she was to him. She had changed so much that he could scarcely believe she was the same woman.

Yet physically she was exactly as he remembered her: the same light, arching brows over blue eyes and pale skin as fine as porcelain; the same slightly upturned nose and golden curls; the same petite form with its generous breasts and tiny waist. During the past three weeks, he had studied her intently for some bodily discrepancy, but could find only intangible ones—spirit and sparkle and wit.

Now the indignation mirrored in her face over the motives of his would-be friends was so transparently genuine that Garth was pleased. He could not resist, however, saying dryly, "It is one of the hazards of being so rich. Men want to be your friend, and women want to be your wife."

His sprite seemed so flustered and distressed by his pointed reminder of her own motive that he felt a little sorry for her.

Finally, she said defensively, "At least I told you my reason. You did not even bother to explain to me why you did not think we would suit."

She deserved an explanation, but he could not tell her the truth: that he had erroneously thought her a colorless, boring ninnyhammer of inferior understanding, who cared only for herself, her clothes, and her parties. No, he could not tell her that because he knew she would be deeply hurt, and he could not bear to do that. Besides it was no longer true.

Instead he said gently, "I fear that when I left for Brazil, you were still more child than woman, and I was under the mistaken impression that you were—er, rather selfish and overconcerned about your health. Clearly you blossomed while I was there, but your letters gave me no clue to the metamorphosis you were undergoing."

Smiling, he took her hands in his. "Why did you write me of nothing except the parties you attended and all those endless descriptions of every gown you wore?"

She seemed, for a moment, to be at a loss for words. Then she said, "I was afraid that you would think me a bluestocking. You wrote that I must take care not to become one."

"I was being sarcastic. I was certain you had never read a book either for knowledge or pleasure." He squeezed her hands affectionately. "How very different you are from your letters."

"So are you," Sally retorted, remembering the one that she had found in the pocket of Serena's redingote. "You sounded like an odious preacher."

He laughed. "You were not meant to like them."

What a wonderful laugh he had, so deep and genuine and infectious. That and the charmingly mischievous look on his handsome face made Sally's heart leap.

"I confess that all my letters were written with the sole object of getting you to cry off. It was easy enough for me to write such letters. I had only to imitate my father's to me."

He smiled lovingly at her. "When I came home, I thought that we would be as ill-matched as my own parents, but I was wrong. You have changed so much the past two years that it is as though you are a different woman."

His smile turned to a frown. "Good God, Sprite, what did I say to make you look so stricken?"

She blushed and stammered, "I . . . I . . . nothing."

Her lips were half-parted in a sensual, but wholly unconscious, invitation. His puzzlement was forgotten in his longing to kiss her. He did so with all the expertise at his command, brushing his lips, then his tongue teasingly over her mouth before deepening the kiss.

She returned it hungrily. The passion of her response startled, even shocked him a little. Yet he was strangely exhilarated by it, too. How different her kisses now were from the reluctant, dutiful pecks she had given him two years ago that had held no pleasure for either of them.

He rubbed her cheek gently with his thumb. Her skin was as soft and velvety as a rose petal, and she smelled of roses, too. Garth wanted to drink in her sweet scent, and he hugged her to him. His body responded at once to the press of her soft curves.

He lifted his head, and she gave an involuntary little moan of protest as his mouth deserted hers.

. What a fascinating creature she was, so innocent and yet so passionate. He was accustomed to sophisticated women. Never before had he been responsible for awakening a maiden's desire, and he found it far more exciting than he had anticipated.

He lowered his lips to hers again, and his hands began moving over her body. Then he left a fiery trail of kisses down her slender neck, collarbone, and the swell of her breasts above the low-cut dress.

Sally tried to protest, but the words died in her throat and only a startled gasp emerged as an intense wave of pleasure washed over her, then receded, and left her aching for she knew not what.

Sally told herself that she must stop him, but she could not immediately overrule the wild yearning of her heart. When she belatedly tried to push Garth away, he said gently, "My darling sprite, there is nothing wrong in this. After all, we are to be married."

Sally stiffened. If only that were true, but it would never happen.

Garth was watching her with puzzled eyes. "What is it, Sprite?"

Emma's voice came from the hall. She had been reading David a bedtime story and must have finished. In a moment, she would come into the drawing room.

Sally pulled away from Garth, but he caught her arms with his hands. In an urgent undertone, he demanded, "Tell me, Sprite, do you still think marriage to me beneath you?"

She could not force herself to lie to him. "No, *I* do not," she admitted.

That was true, she thought miserably, but marriage to Sally Marlowe, strolling player, would be very much beneath Garth, and he would despise her when he learned how she had deceived him.

14

The heat, instead of abating the following day, intensified. Even in late afternoon, it was oppressively hot and sticky on the shaded terrace of Wycombe Abbey where Emma and Sally were sitting. Not a hint of a breeze stirred the still, humid air.

Emma waved a circular fan on ivory sticks vigorously before her face in a futile attempt to cool herself. Her soft, compassionate eyes studied her companion. "Poor dear, you look as exhausted as I feel."

Dark half-circles beneath Sally's eyes attested to the sleepless night she had spent. It had not been the temperature that had kept her awake though, but roiling emotions and a beleagured conscience. She could no longer deny that she was hopelessly in love with Garth. The longer she remained at Wycombe Abbey, the more devastating the end, when it finally came, would be.

This miserable charade had to be ended immediately. But how? The only time that Garth had come near to crying off was when she had horrified him by wearing breeches and riding bareback. Sally had to think of something so outrageous that he would be shocked into breaking the engagement.

Emma, still fanning herself, suggested, "You should try to nap."

"Yes, I believe I will," Sally replied. She did not want sleep, however, but solitude in which to think.

Upstairs in Serena's bedroom, Sally began to pace the floor, the petticoats of her jonquil-yellow gown clinging damply to her legs. She longed for a cooling swim, but when she had inquired of Jane whether Serena had a bathing dress, the maid had said that her delicate mistress would not dream of putting so much as a toe into any body of water larger than a bathtub.

Sally was thankful that she had grown up in the freedom of a theatrical family that considered strictures against such exercise for girls to be nonsense. Her brother had taught her to swim when she was a child, and it remained one of her favorite recreations. Now, the cool waters of the pond where Garth had discovered her in breeches tempted Sally.

Suddenly, inspiration struck her as to how she could sink herself beneath reproach in Garth's eyes.

Hastily, she pulled her breeches on under her petticoats, then changed out of her fragile yellow sandals into a pair of half-boots more suitable for walking. She donned a wide-brimmed straw bonnet tied with ribbons that matched the jonquil-yellow of her muslin gown.

Telling no one where she was bound, she slipped out of the house and set off on foot at a brisk pace for the pond.

It was a long walk, but Sally dared not ask for a horse from the stable. The head groom would insist that one of his men accompany her, and she had to be alone for what she planned.

By the time she reached the pond, she was so hot that it looked as inviting to her as an oasis in the desert.

She was much relieved that she had arrived before Garth rode by it on his way to call upon her. Sally knew he always took the path past the pond when he came to Wycombe Abbey, and he was due to arrive there any time now. She prayed that no one else would happen by, but she must take that chance.

Hiding behind a clump of willow saplings, she shed her gown, revealing her breeches that she had concealed beneath her skirts and her thin lawn chemise.

To ensure that Garth did not miss her in the pond, she hung her bright yellow gown and its petticoats on the alders along the path where it curved closest to the water. Then she made her way through the loosestrife and meadowsweet.

At the pond's edge, she removed her half-boots and tied the skirt of her chemise around her waist, wishing that its thin lawn material was heavier. Although Sally was an actress used to quick costume changes, she was modest enough to be unnerved by the thought of Garth's eyes upon her in it. She would have to remain submerged beneath the water's protective cover and stubbornly refuse to emerge from it until he left.

Before her courage failed her, she dove into the water.

After the heat of the day, it felt wonderful. She surfaced and swam rapidly toward the opposite shore of the pond and back again. Then she turned over and floated on her back.

Garth rode at a rapid clip along his private path to Wycombe Abbey. He could hardly wait to see his sprite again. Her passionate response to him the previous night had quieted both his concern that she would be marrying him only for his fortune and his lingering doubts about shackling himself to a hoyden.

He smiled proudly to himself. He had set out to win her heart, and he was certain he had succeeded.

Although he always dressed with care, he had taken special pains before leaving Tamar this afternoon to look his best for his betrothed. She had been his father's selection for his bride. Now, at last, she was his own choice as well, and it was time to let her know that. He intended to propose formally to her today.

In preparation for this momentous occasion, he had ordered his valet to lay out the new forest-green coat by Weston that had arrived only yesterday from London and a newly acquired pair of Hoby's finest boots that he had not yet worn.

Garth had tied, then discarded nearly a dozen neck-cloths before he achieved the perfection he desired, despite his valet's sincere assurance that every one of those rejected attempts should have made even the most demanding pink of the *ton* happy.

As he rode along the path that skirted the pond, he could scarcely believe his eyes when he saw the yellow gown and petticoats hanging like flags from the willows. He did not, however, have the smallest doubt whose garments they were.

"What the devil," he muttered, half out of the saddle before his horse stopped.

Plunging through the loosestrife and meadowsweet, he saw to his horror that his betrothed was lying face-up in the water, several yards from the bank. Since ladies who could swim were an unknown species to him, he drew the only conclusion that he could. She had somehow tumbled in and could not save herself.

Terrified that he was already too late to save her, Garth ran toward the water's edge, shedding his new Weston coat as he went. Already she had drifted too far out for him to reach her from shore, and he jumped into the water without taking the time to remove his boots.

His powerful strokes brought him quickly to her. He grabbed her with the intention of towing her to the safety of the bank when she began struggling against him, pulling them both under the water.

Choking and sputtering, he regained the surface. At least she was still alive, but clearly she was in such panic that she did not know what she was doing.

He was half-right. Sally was panicked, but she knew very well what she was doing. It had never occurred to her that Garth would attempt to pull her from beneath the water's concealing cover where she had expected to remain until after he had left. Now, realizing his intent, she desperately tried to stop him.

"Dammit, Sprite, stop fighting me!" he sputtered. "What the devil are you trying to do—drown us both?"

"What are *you* trying to do?"

"Save you, you ninnyhammer."

"I don't want to be saved," she wailed.

It was, however, too late. He had reached the shallow water along the bank. Planting his feet on the muddy bottom, he hauled her up into his arms and staggered from the pond.

He laid her on the bank, but she scrambled hastily to her feet. To his astonishment, she would have thrown herself back into the water if he had not grabbed her arm, hauling her back.

"What the devil are you doing—trying to drown yourself?" he demanded angrily.

"I am swimming," she said with soggy dignity.

He was amazed that she knew how. Water was dripping from her bedraggled golden curls, and his gaze followed these rivulets downward to the wet lawn of her chemise plastered to her body in a way that was somehow even more revealing than if she had been naked. An insatiable hunger for her surged through him at the sight of her firm young breasts with their rosebud tips pressing against the thin material.

Angry at her outrageous behavior and embarrassed by his body's uncontrollable reaction to it, he grabbed his handsome, abominably expensive new coat. Without an instant's hesitation, Garth draped it over her. He suppressed an anguished groan as he saw the water stains spreading like fungus on the fine material.

Never had he known a young lady of quality to act in such a disgraceful manner, swimming half-naked in public for all the world to see! He was too angry to recollect that he was the only one who regularly used this path.

Her conduct was beyond the pale. He was so scandalized by it that he rescinded his decision to marry her.

He thought of the ideal wife he had dreamed of: quiet, demure, submissive to his wishes, with pretty manners. In short, a lady who was impeccably proper in both speech and behavior.

Dammit, she was none of these things.

"Have . . . have I sunk myself beneath reproach in your eyes?" she inquired, her voice suddenly husky and an odd mixture of hope and pain in her brilliant eyes.

"Yes!" he thundered. He could not, would not marry such an outrageous hoyden, and he bluntly told her so.

"I . . . I can understand why you would feel as you do." She looked as though she were about to burst into tears. "I know that I am a grave disappointment to you, but I am what I am," she said with a profound sadness that wrenched at his heart. "We must find Thorley."

"Why?"

"So that you can tell him you are ending our betrothal."

He studied her suspiciously. For a girl who professed to want to marry him, she was accepting his decision with remarkable calm. He had the uneasy feeling that he had walked headlong into a trap. Yet he did not doubt that she cared deeply for him.

Perhaps she was as confused in her feelings toward him as he was toward her.

Droplets glistened on her lovely face, and water still dripped from her curls onto the shoulders of his ruined coat. He made the mistake of looking lower. His jacket hung open, and he gritted his teeth against the almost overwhelming desire to thrust his hands beneath it and caress those rosy-tipped breasts that were as sweet and tempting as Eve's apple.

Through clenched jaw, he demanded, "What the devil possessed you to go into the water like this?"

She met his gaze defiantly. "I was merely following your advice. You wrote me that I should take cold baths in a creek to harden my delicate health."

"Good God, I never thought you would heed me!"

"Do you mean that you would not have advised me

so if you thought that I would?'' she asked innocently. ''I do not understand.''

At this point, neither did Garth. He was shaken by the ungentlemanly urges that she aroused in him. It was all he could do to keep from peeling his jacket off her delectable little body and making her his own.

Cursing silently, he took a step toward her. His foot squished in his waterlogged boot, and its back seam split. His foot came out of the ruined leather.

''You are damnably hard on my wardrobe,'' he said ruefully as he looked down on himself. His shirt and the perfectly tied neckcloth upon which he had lavished such care were sodden messes. His buckskin breeches felt as though they were shrinking on him even as he talked. His new boots were a total loss.

''You should choose a better boot-maker,'' she advised.

''Hoby himself made these boots!'' he exclaimed, much affronted. ''There is no more sought-after boot-maker.''

She shrugged, a teasing gleam in her eyes. ''That is what you get for patronizing an inferior boot-maker just because he is all the crack.''

He could not help laughing at that, even though he was outraged by her latest escapade. Sobering, he demanded, ''Have you no shame?''

''No,'' she retorted, but she looked embarrassed, and her response lacked her usual fire. ''I am well covered.''

''Are you?'' he demanded scathingly.

She followed his gaze downward to where his ruined coat gaped open on her. A horrified little gasp escaped her lips, and a bright red flood of color surged up her body. Hastily, she grabbed the front of his coat and clutched it around her as though she were suddenly in danger of freezing.

Garth realized that she had not known how revealing her wet chemise was. His anger evaporated, and he was seized by a baffling desire to take her in his arms and comfort her. Once again the battle that he had thought he had won erupted in his heart.

Good God, had he taken leave of his senses?

He was a rational, logical man, and she was not at all what he wanted in a wife.

Any rational, logical man should be appalled by her.

He was appalled by her.

Yet, dammit, he wanted her as he had never before wanted a woman.

15

While Garth waited by the pond, Sally, well concealed from his sight behind a screen of bushes, stripped off her wet chemise and breeches. Silent tears slipped down her cheeks. In vain did she try to tell herself that she should be delighted. She had gotten Garth to cry off, bringing an abrupt end to this miserable charade. But it was the most bitter and painful success of her life. Now she would leave Wycombe Abbey, perhaps this very night.

Serena, freed of her unwanted betrothal, would resume her rightful place in her brother's home. Sally would never see Garth again.

As she dried herself with a cloth she had brought from the Abbey for that purpose, the tears trickling down her cheeks became a cascade. Never again would Garth's strong arms embrace her, his mouth possess hers, his touch tease her. No other man had ever ignited that strange yearning in her and, she thought bleakly, no other man would ever be able to satisfy it.

Garth's thoughts, meanwhile, were no less confused. Although the sprite was well hidden from him, her rustlings as she changed into her yellow muslin gown and petticoats inspired such vivid images in his mind that he very nearly had to resort to another plunge into the cold pond.

The ride back to Wycombe Abbey was equally torturous for him. Because she had walked to the pond, he was obliged to carry her crossways before him on his saddle. He had to endure the tantalizing press and rub of her hip against him.

In truth, he was so baffled by his feelings for her that he no longer knew his own mind. Her provoking tongue and abominable want of conduct shocked him. Yet the thought of not seeing her again, of never making love to her, of never exploring the depths of the passion between them, plunged him into black despair.

He must be touched in the upper works, he thought glumly.

By the time they reached the Abbey, Garth was trying desperately to think of an excuse to postpone ending his betrothal until he could sort out his confused feelings for Serena.

When they had dismounted, he handed the reins of his horse to a groom who stood gawking at them.

Garth could not blame the poor man. What a sight they must make. His sprite looked the picture of a demure, proper young lady in her jonquil-yellow gown and wide-brimmed straw bonnet with its bright ribbons. She had hidden her damp curls, the only remaining sign that she had been in the pond, under the bonnet.

He, on the other hand, had no dry clothes to change into, and water still dripped from him. Although Garth was no fop, his dress was always impeccable, and he was mortifyingly aware of what a sorry appearance he presented: disheveled, soaking wet, and shuffling along in a ruined, waterlogged boot.

As the groom led the big bay away, Thorley rushed out from the house. "Good God, Garth, what a sight you are! You look like you met with an accident. Did you fall into the pond?"

"No," Garth snapped, "I jumped in."

Thorley raised his eyebrows. "With all your clothes on? How very odd of you!"

Before Garth could explain his peculiar behavior, the

sprite said, "He has decided to end our engagement, Thor."

Garth wanted to throttle her. It was no longer true, and now he had to find a way to say he had changed his mind without looking like an indecisive fool. He began diplomatically, "I cannot bear to subject Serena to the public humiliation that my jilting her would surely bring her, so I—"

"Oh, no, you won't!" Thorley interrupted. "You are dicked in the nob if you think I am so flat I shall let you get away with that. I am awake to your scheme."

Garth, who had intended to say that he was not breaking the engagement after all, demanded in astonishment, "What the devil are you talking about?"

"You want to tell the world that Serena jilted you," Thorley cried hotly, "so that you can demand repayment of all the money that my father borrowed from yours because she has done so!"

Garth had not even thought of those loans, nor had it been his intention to seek payment of them. He stared incredulously at the young earl. "I am astonished that those loans, rather than your sister's happiness and reputation, should be your first concern," Garth told him bluntly. "I never thought you such a lick-penny."

Thorley flushed angrily. "Takes one to know one," he muttered rashly under his breath.

That utterly untrue charge made Garth every bit as irate as the earl. He had many faults but he was not clutch-fisted, as Thorley should well know. Had he not paid Serena's exhorbitant expenses for her come-out, including the bills for enough gowns to clothe half of London, without a murmur of protest? It had all been quite improper but the late earl had demanded it, saying he had not the blunt to outfit his daughter properly.

Garth said with icy fury, "If that is what you think, perhaps I shall oblige your opinion of me by insisting upon repayment of the money."

The color receded from Thorley's face. "You cannot.

The agreements stipulated that if you cried off, the loans must be forgiven.''

The earl had unwittingly provided Garth with the excuse that he had been looking for. He shrugged carelessly. "Then I shall not cry off."

The consternation on Thorley's face was comical, but Garth was not amused. It strengthened his growing suspicion that the earl very much wanted the engagement ended—but at no cost to himself. Garth wondered angrily whether Wycombe thought a mere baronet was not good enough for his sister. If that were the case, Garth would be damned if he would enrich him by forgiving the loans.

Thorley started to protest, "But you said—"

Garth cut him off. "I have changed my mind." He paused before adding significantly, "At least for now."

He had bought himself time to resolve his confused feelings while reserving the option of calling off the marriage in the future.

Having achieved that, he turned to bid his fiancée good-bye so that he could go home and change out of his ruined clothes.

Garth was startled to see how miserable she looked. He wondered bitterly whether it was because of her brother's behavior or because she was still engaged to him. His lips curled in a grim little smile. "Good day, *my betrothed.*"

"But . . . you . . . said I was not at all what you want in a wife." She was struggling to hold back the tears glistening in her eyes.

"Don't tell me you are at last having second thoughts about marrying me?" he asked sarcastically. "Only think of my great fortune!"

"I . . . I have come to agree with you that there can be no happiness when a husband does not respect his wife," she said humbly. A single tear rolled down her cheek.

She looked so unhappy that he could not stop his wayward heart from weakening. He gently brushed the tear away from her soft, pale cheek. "Perhaps you could convince me that I should," he said gravely.

"But you despise my hoydenish behavior." Her voice faltered and her gaze fell away from his.

"Yes, but there are other things about you that I like." At least she would not bore him to death, which had been his original fear.

Her beautiful face stared up at him questioningly, her eyes awash in unshed tears.

Beyond a doubt, he thought triumphantly, the proud Lady Serena had come to care for her insignificant baronet.

Garth bent his head and kissed her tenderly.

Then, with a glowing smile, he said softly, "Goodbye, my Sprite."

After Garth was gone, Sally turned on Thorley, unleashing her pent-up misery and despair. "At last, I got him to cry off, and you ruined everything! How could you have been such a cod's head as to set up his back like that?"

"My damnable temper got the best of me. God help me, I have made a terrible mull of the whole affair!"

Thorley looked as tired and drawn as Sally felt. The sad, pinched set of his face told her that he, too, was deeply sorry and much worried about the events he had set in motion. Her anger at him faded. She felt sorry for him.

And sorry for them all.

She feared they would pay a very high price for their deception.

"I have always liked Garth, always regarded him as a friend," Thorley said sadly, "but he will never forgive me for this."

"What shall we do?"

His dark eyes were bleak. "I tried to contact my banker to ask for a loan so I can repay Garth, but he is away from London on holiday. I have an appointment with him when he returns next week."

"Do you think he will oblige you?"

"I don't know," Thorley admitted. "I tried to borrow the blunt from him after Papa died, and he refused. But I have done so much in the past year to restore the estate that perhaps now he will listen to me. If he does, I will tell Garth the truth immediately."

And what would happen then?

Her heart revolted at the answer. She loved Garth too much to lose him forever. And she was certain that he had, albeit most reluctantly, come to love her, too.

They would be so right and happy together, but he was too proud to marry a lowly strolling player.

A mad, desperate scheme took shape in Sally's mind.

If only she could make Garth love her so much that when he learned the truth he would accept her in place of Serena.

It was an ignoble plan.

She was contemptible even to consider it.

Yet she loved Garth so much.

She must at least try.

16

During the week that followed, Sally maintained the decorum of an angel. Garth said nothing more about breaking their engagement but neither did he mention setting a wedding date. He did not, however, act like a man who was about to jilt her.

On the morning that Thorley was to leave for London, Sally was alone with Emma in the breakfast parlor when the countess asked suddenly, "You are in love with Garth, aren't you?"

"Yes," Sally admitted.

Emma took Sally's hand in her own, squeezing it comfortingly. "He loves you, too. Perhaps he will still marry you after he learns the truth."

It was what Sally prayed for. She had even managed to convince herself that he would, but in her heart of hearts she was terrified that she was deluding herself.

Emma said hopefully, "He never liked Serena, and he is daft over you."

"You are the one who is daft," Thorley told his wife. He had slipped unnoticed into the breakfast parlor as the two women talked. "You females are foolish romantics. Garth is far too toplofty to marry an actress."

Sally's hopes plummeted at Thorley's candid assessment. Much as she wanted to believe he was wrong, she feared he was not.

He said bluntly, "Your only hope of getting Garth to

145

the altar is to marry him before he learns that you are not Serena.''

"Infamous!" Sally exclaimed, horrified. "Despicable! I love Garth too much to do that to him."

"Yes, it would be despicable," Thorley agreed, "but it is the only way you will get him to marry you."

Emma interjected, "What would happen when Serena reappeared and Garth learned that he had been tricked into marriage to an impostor?"

Sally shuddered. "He would be justified in murdering me!"

"Yes," the earl said, "the only thing that would save you is my insisting that Serena is the impostor."

"You could not do that to your own sister!" Sally cried.

"No, I could not, although God knows it would be no more than she deserved for acting as she has and getting us all into this cruel coil."

"You should have told Garth immediately that Serena had run away rather than marry him," Sally said. "I am persuaded that he would have forgiven the loans, but now . . ."

"Yes, I know," Thorley said grimly. "One more in a long line of stupid mistakes I have made. I pray that I can persuade my banker to loan me the blunt to pay Garth off. Whatever the outcome of my meeting with him, we must go to Garth as soon as I get back and tell him the truth."

"Yes, we must," Sally agreed, although it would take all her courage to do so. "The sooner the better. Perhaps I should do so before—"

"No, don't even think of it!" he interrupted. "You are not to tell him until I am with you. He will be murderously angry. Garth rarely loses his temper, but when he does . . ." Thorley looked shaken by the prospect. "I will only be gone until the day after tomorrow. Swear to me, Sally, that you will wait until my return."

When she did not respond, he pleaded, "Do so for my sake, as well as yours. Garth would think me a

contemptible coward if I let you face him alone. Whatever chance I have of reasoning with him would be lost.
Give me your oath that you will wait for me.''

Thorley was so insistent that Sally did. It would not
matter if another day or two went by before Garth
learned the truth.

Garth was alone with his sprite in the drawing room
of Wycombe Abbey. Thorley was in London on some
mysterious errand, and Emma had gone upstairs to say
good night to David.

Studying his fiancée, Garth could not help smiling to
himself. She looked like such a sweet, innocent, genteel girl, in her high-necked gown of sprig muslin. Nor
could he complain of her conduct since he had pulled
her from the pond a week ago. She had been a pattern
card of propriety. It was clear that she was trying hard
to please him and that did please him—very much.

With her as his wife, he thought, he would at last
enjoy living at Tamar. Her presence would imbue that
big stone pile with a warmth it had not had before. He
looked forward eagerly to the family that they would
create together, golden-haired girls and green-eyed
boys.

Yes, it was time to set their wedding date, and he
told her so.

For a fleeting instant, her eyes had the look of a
trapped animal.

"But . . . but you told me I was not at all what you
wanted in a wife," she faltered.

"I was wrong about what I wanted."

So very wrong. He recalled with rueful amusement
the wife he had thought he desired: quiet, demure, submissive, beautifully behaved, a woman who would
never dream of challenging him.

But his sprite did challenge him. He belatedly realized that her questioning of silly strictures and her ebullient, free spirit, unlike that of any other woman he had
known, enchanted him more than it outraged him.

He liked to discuss his ideas with her, too, because she had a good deal of common sense, and he valued her suggestions.

Most important of all, he could confide in her as he had never been able to do before with anyone, male or female.

He was still incredulous over the remarkable—indeed, miraculous—change in her during the past two years. Garth had not thought it possible for a person to alter that drastically, but he had seen enough of her the past few weeks to be assured that her transformation was genuine.

No longer able to withstand the temptation of her irresistible mouth, he kissed her, gently at first and then with growing passion.

Sally returned his kiss hungrily, beset by all those aching yearnings that he never failed to arouse in her.

His mouth deserted her lips and moved caressingly over her face and down her neck.

She moaned with pleasure. He knew how to make love charmingly. Such skill did not come without experience. A man as rich and charming as he could have had many mistresses. Jealously lashed Sally at the thought of Garth with another woman.

She remembered the speculative gleam of interest in his eyes that day he had met her in her Cleopatra costume. Was he one of those men she so disliked who frequented the greenrooms of theaters, buying comely actresses' favors? Before she could stop her incorrigible tongue, she had given voice to this question.

His jaw dropped. "Sprite, that is a most improper thing to ask me! How would you even know of such things?"

Her chin rose defiantly. "Is it not what gentlemen often do?"

"Not this gentleman," he said with dignity. "Whatever my other failings, Sprite, I know my own worth, and I do not seek my—er, recreation among the lower orders."

His answer hit Sally with the force of a lightning bolt. The small flicker of hope deep in her heart that he would still want to marry her after he knew the truth was extinguished.

Thorley was right. She had been deluding herself. A man of Garth's pride would never marry her once he learned her real identity.

Yet she was certain that they could be very happy together.

Her anguish turned to anger, and suddenly she was furious at him and his foolish pride. So long as he thought that she had the title of "Lady" before her name he would be delighted to marry her. Without that, even though she was the same person, he would not even deign to make her his mistress.

"You are worse than I am!" Sally cried, trying to blink back the tears of indignation and despair collecting in her eyes. "You were angry that I should think my future husband beneath me socially, but you . . . you would not even stoop to choose a convenient who is beneath you!"

She turned away, no longer able to hold back her tears, and fled from the room.

her as his wife. It would not matter to him that Sally loved him more than she had thought it possible for her
.....

17

~~~~~~~~~~~~~~~~~~~

Sally and Emma were in the breakfast parlor, lingering over their tea. Not until Thorley arrived back from London at midday would they know whether he had been successful with his banker.

The doors to the arbor were open, and a breeze scented with roses wafted into the room. Sally, breathing deeply of it, wished again that her mother could see this beautiful, peaceful spot. How she would love it.

Mama would have received Sally's letter by now telling that she was at Wycombe Abbey. Her mother must have been astonished when she saw the earl's frank on it and even more staggered when, reading its contents, she learned that her daughter was residing temporarily in his country house.

Sally had dared not confess to Mama the real reason she was at Wycombe Abbey. Instead she had written that the Wycombes had kindly offered her shelter after she had been refused a room at the only inn in Aveton (that much, at least, was true), then urged her to remain with them for a while before she went to Bath.

A lump swelled in Sally's throat. She would be on her way to Bath very quickly after Thorley's return from London. Once they told Garth the truth, there would be no reason for her to remain. He would have nothing more to do with her. A man who considered it beneath him to make an actress his mistress would never accept her as his wife. It would not matter to him that Sally loved him more than she had thought it possible for her to love anyone.

Tears gathered in her eyes. She would miss Emma and Thorley and little David dreadfully, but leaving Garth behind would be like tearing her heart out. The thought of never seeing him again filled her with bleak despair, and she brushed away a tear from her eye.

Emma, guessing the reason for it, said sympathetically, "My poor dear." She patted Sally's hand comfortingly. "I wish you were my sister-in-law. I like you so much, and Serena has made our lives so difficult the past year. It was as though she was determined to be as disagreeable as she possibly could."

"What happened between Serena and her father that caused her to change?"

Emma hesitated. Sally feared that the countess would again refuse to tell her, but after a moment she said, "They had a thundering quarrel. It ended with Serena running from the room, screaming that she hated him. He came out after her, his face purple with rage. A short while later he suffered a stroke that left him mute and paralyzed, and he died three days later."

Horrified, Sally cried, "What did they fight about?"

"Not even Thorley could get out of Serena what happened. I only know that she had gone to him to say she would not marry Garth."

"Because she wanted to wed Lord Leland?"

"No, she did not become involved with Lee until later. But that dreadful Netta Bridger had already convinced her that Garth was beneath her."

"And her father insisted she must wed Garth?"

"Undoubtedly he did, but he must have told her something else that overset her. I have never seen her in such a state." Emma closed her eyes as though trying to shut out unhappy memories. "After that, she seemed determined to make everyone around her as miserable as she clearly was."

"But she must have felt dreadful when her father died."

Emma's mouth tightened. "She said that she was glad."

Sally gasped.

"She was in such a flame at the time that I do not think she truly meant it. But that quarrel with my father-in-law altered her radically."

As Garth rode toward Wycombe Abbey, he saw a flash of turquoise emerge from the side of the house and move into the rose arbor. He prayed that it was his sprite for he urgently wanted to be private with her.

Instead of presenting himself at the front door, he hurried around to the side. He found her in the arbor, her back to him, bent over a red rose in full bloom.

To Garth's relief, Emma was nowhere in sight, and he knew that Thorley was not expected back from London until later in the day. Garth would get his wish to be alone with his sprite.

For a moment, he watched her silently, admiring her beauty and aching to make love to her. But he would be gentleman enough to wait until their wedding day.

If only she would set it.

Why had she evaded doing so the previous night, then fled from him in tears? He had been baffled by her reluctance to name a date until a letter arrived that morning from his aunt in London. Its contents had sent him scowling down the path to Wycombe Abbey.

When Garth wished his sprite a good morning, her hand fell away from the rose she had been examining. She straightened and faced him. The surprise and unmistakable delight in her eyes at the sight of him calmed a little the anxiety that had been gnawing at him since he had read his aunt's letter.

"I did not expect to see you this morning," she said in her lovely flutelike voice that so pleased him.

"I had to talk to you." He led her to an oak bench nestled amid the roses.

She smiled. "Have you thought of some new scheme to improve Tamar?"

"No, I want to know why you avoided setting our wedding date last night," he said bluntly.

The question clearly caught her by surprise. It was a moment before she answered. "I . . . I am not persuaded that I am the wife you want."

"Are you certain you do not have another reason for refusing to name a date?"

Her blue eyes widened, and he thought he saw a flash of fear in them.

"What other reason could I have?" she asked.

"Lord Leland Caine."

Garth's heart sank at the expression on her face. "How stricken you look. So there is something to the gossip."

"What gossip?"

"I had a letter from my aunt today. She wrote that you were trying to fix Lee's interest this past season. You and he are now the subject of considerable speculation."

He paused, hoping that she would deny it all, but she only looked unhappily at the ground.

Garth was suddenly furious. He would have been angry had she been interested in any other man. But good God, *Leland Caine!* What could a woman of his sprite's intelligence see in that silly nodcock? Among the men's clubs in London, Lee was well known to be an indolent, although good-natured, slowtop. Beau Brummell was widely quoted as saying that talking to Lord Leland was like trying to converse with a tree stump—and a good deal less interesting.

"My aunt says London is agog with the rumor that you have eloped with Lee."

"*What!*" Her head snapped up.

Garth's anger faded at the horrified look on her face.

"Clearly that is not true or you would not be sitting here," he conceded. "But do you have a *tendre* for him?"

Her gaze met his squarely. "No, *I* do not."

"Then let us set our wedding date."

She looked as though she were about to burst into tears. In a broken voice, she asked, "Garth, please tell me something. Why did you not break our engagement when you first came home? You wanted to, but instead you tried to get me to do it."

He said impatiently, "Surely, Sprite, you know the answer to that as well as I do."

Sally had accepted Thorley's belief that it had been because Garth wanted the loans repaid, but nothing else about his behavior supported his being a pinch-purse. He was expending large sums without a quibble on improving his land and his tenants' lot at Tamar. Had Thorley been as wrong about Garth's motive in not crying off as he had about what would get him to do so?

"Can it be you don't know, Sprite? What did you think my reason was?"

"You . . . you wanted Thor to have to repay the loans from your father."

He stiffened with anger. "What a muckworm you and your brother think me! Those damned loans had nothing to do with it." He gave a bitter little laugh. "If I was such a nip-cheese, why would I have paid the exorbitant expenses of your come-out season without a murmur?"

"What?" Sally cried, staggered. Why had Thorley never told her that? She had wondered how the late earl in his straitened financial circumstances had been able to pay for all those gowns in Serena's overflowing closet. "How very improper!" Although she was not awake to all the quality's odd notions of propriety, she knew that much.

"So your papa did not tell you," Garth said grimly. "What's more, when I returned from Brazil, I seriously considered telling your brother that I would forgive the loans if you would agree to end the betrothal."

Sally swallowed hard. If only Garth had done so,

they would not be in this terrible coil now. "Why didn't you?"

"I thought he would be grossly insulted—justifiably so—by my trying to buy my way out of our betrothal."

"But why bother? Why not simply tell Thorley that you no longer wished to marry me?"

"You know as well as I do that it is beyond the pale for a man of honor to break his betrothal to a lady."

No, Sally did not know. Another one of the quality's queer starts that made no sense to her. She protested, "It is ridiculous that a gentleman cannot break an engagement to a lady with whom he won't suit!"

Garth said grimly, "But he should have ascertained that before he made his offer."

"But you did not make the offer. Your father did."

"True, but I was bound."

"What if I had told you when you came home that I, too, wanted to cry off but could not do so because Thorley could not repay the loans?"

"Good God, Sprite, I would have considered forgiving them, a cheap price to escape an ill-suited marriage." Garth smiled at her. "But it does not signify now, for I am persuaded that we will suit very well indeed." Then his smiled turned to a frown. "What's wrong, Sprite? You look positively ill."

She was. Nausea convulsed her stomach. Sally despised herself. She had been so wrong about Garth in the beginning, misreading his character totally. It was all Sally could do to keep from bursting into tears of shame when she thought of how she had lied and deceived him. A man of his honor would be shocked and revolted—and rightfully so—when he learned the hoax that had been perpetrated on him.

"Oh, Garth," she cried, a sob in her voice, "you deserve better than me. I will not make you a proper wife."

"That is for me to decide, Sprite," he said, taking her face gently between his hands and kissing her with aching tenderness.

When he raised his lips from hers, the love in his eyes was like a knife in Sally's heart.

He smiled possessively down at her. "You are the wife I want, and I know that you want me."

After that kiss, she could not deny it.

His fingertips stroked her face. "Do you love me, Sprite?"

"More than words can tell," she answered truthfully.

The elation in his eyes broke her heart.

He said huskily, "Then we shall set our wedding date now."

This was the moment to tell him the truth, but Sally was bound by her oath to Thorley that she would not do so until he returned from London. Nevertheless, she vowed to her nagging conscience, the sun would not set on this day without Garth knowing the truth.

Hastily she said, "Thor insists on being a party to setting the date. I promise you that I shall bring him to Tamar as soon as he returns from London."

Garth frowned. "But—"

"Please, there is something we must discuss with you. Then we will set the date if it is what you still want."

Sally struggled to hold back her tears. Garth would not want it, of course. Not once he knew the truth.

He would despise her for hoaxing him, despise her even more for tricking him into loving a woman he considered so far beneath him.

"If it is what I still want," Garth repeated quizzically. Then his lips claimed hers again.

Sally gave herself up to his kiss, savoring it, trying to imprint the memory of it forever in her mind, knowing that it would be the last she would ever have from him.

When he raised his head, he smiled at her, his eyes full of love. The searing pain in her heart robbed her of breath. Once he knew the truth, he would have only hatred and contempt for her.

"If it is what I still want?" Garth echoed again. "You already have your answer on that point, my Sprite."

But it was not the answer he thought.

18

When Garth left Wycombe Abbey, he took a circuitous route home so that he could check on the housing he was having built. His sprite's puzzling words nagged at him: *"We will set the date if it is what you still want."* Try as he might, he could not put them from his mind.

Why on earth would she think he might not want it? He suspected that Thorley planned to demand additional blunt to ease his financial difficulties in exchange for his sister's hand. Did she fear that her brother would make such exorbitant demands on him that he would renege?

When Garth belatedly reached Tamar, a closed carriage was parked in front of the entrance. Thorley must have returned early from London. Garth's spirits soared at how promptly Serena had kept her word to bring him to Tamar. Then a closer look at the equipage told him it was not Wycombe's. He cursed silently. The last thing he wanted now was to entertain surprise callers.

His butler, Renton, his face a study of majestic disapproval, informed his master that his visitor, a young lady, awaited him in the state drawing room.

Thinking his caller was Serena after all, Garth wondered whether Thorley had acquired a new carriage while he was in London. But why had Renton shown Serena into the state drawing room instead of the informal, much more inviting room he now used for that purpose?

"Is Lord Wycombe with her?" Garth asked.

"No, sir," his butler replied woodenly.

"She came alone?" Garth wondered why Thorley had not come with her after all.

"No, sir. She is accompanied by her maid."

Renton gave the very slightest of nods toward a prim, branfaced girl, sitting rigidly on one of the hall banquettes. She definitely was not Serena's maid, Jane.

Garth frowned. "I thought my caller was Lady Serena."

"No, sir. The young person's name is Netta Bridger."

It had a familiar ring to Garth, although he could not immediately place it. Respectable young ladies, with or without their maids, however, did not call uninvited at the country homes of bachelors, especially those they did not know. "Who the devil is she?"

Renton, an exemplary butler, was reputed never to forget a name or face. "I recollect, sir, that when you were home two years ago she called here with Lady Serena and Lord and Lady Wycombe. She was their guest at Wycombe Abbey and, I believe, a bosom-bow of your betrothed."

Garth hazily recalled a most annoying young female who had attached herself to him whenever he had called at the abbey, but he could not even remember what she looked like.

"But Lady Serena is not with this Miss Bridger now?"

"No, sir."

"How peculiar."

"Yes, sir, very peculiar," his butler agreed.

Garth went into the ornate drawing room that he so detested. He bit back a groan of exasperation when he saw the young lady awaiting him on one of the straight-backed red settees. He did remember her now, not from two years ago but from the recent week he had spent in London after his return from Brazil.

She was that odious, encroaching female who had seemed to be everywhere he turned that week and had been shockingly forward in engaging his attention. At first, he had cursed his monumental ill luck to be seated next to her at four different dinners. Then he belatedly perceived that luck had most likely had nothing to do with it.

Several times he had caught her watching him with a calculating look in her eyes that warned him she was not to be trusted.

Many men no doubt would think her pretty. She had a statuesque figure and a heart-shaped face framed by dark brown hair. Her features were unexceptional except for a protruding pair of gray eyes. But she was one of those managing bluestockings whom he so disliked. Her mind was humorless and pedantic, and she had bored him with parroted opinions that clearly she did not fully understand.

He was far too well bred, however, to let her guess his true feelings about her, and he had politely conversed with her whenever they met, which was at every social engagement he attended.

Strange that she had not mentioned in London that she was Serena's friend. Or had she? Her conversation had been such a dead bore that he realized guiltily he had frequently only appeared to listen to her.

Now that his memory had been jogged, he vaguely recalled her mentioning having met him two years earlier. They had been interrupted just then, and since he had not any recollection of her, he had not pursued the subject.

Greeting her now, he had difficulty disguising his dismay at finding her in his home. "I am sorry that you have been kept waiting," he said with a coolness that negated this apology. "Had I expected you, I would have endeavored to be here."

"It does not signify," she said, ignoring his subtle

request for an explanation of her uninvited appearance. "I was happy to have the opportunity to look about this room. I declare I think it so elegant."

Her taste appalled Garth.

When he came into the room, she had been squirming on the straight-backed settee that Garth had always suspected came from a medieval torture chamber. He could not resist saying mendaciously, "And the settees are exceedingly comfortable, too, don't you agree?"

"Oh, yes, most comfortable," she assured him.

"What brings you to Kent?"

Netta sighed dolefully. "Lady Serena begged me to come."

Why had Serena said nothing to him about asking her friend to visit?

Netta, twisting her features into an expression that approximated sorrow and distaste, said, "Had I known, however, what Serena had done, I should not have come."

Garth observed that Miss Bridger was not a very good actress.

"I assure you, Sir Garth, that I was outraged to have her try to involve me in her reprehensible plot."

Utterly bewildered as to what she could be talking about, he said politely, "I understand that you and my betrothed are bosom-bows."

What he could not understand was why Serena would have anything to do with this peculiar female.

"No, no, not are! *Were!*" she cried dramatically. "Now that I have learned how vilely she has treated you I can no longer be her friend. I was shocked, truly shocked. Indeed, my heart breaks for you!"

This outburst sounded far too well rehearsed to be either spontaneous or heartfelt. Garth eyed her with deep distrust.

"I fear I must be excessively dim-witted today, Miss Bridger, but I cannot immediately perceive why you have come to Tamar, especially without Lady Serena."

Netta, swelling with righteous indignation, cried, "I

have come because I cannot let her deceive you any longer! Oh, Garth, you deserve better than that unfaithful creature—so much better! You deserve a wife who loves you, who wants you, who will make your happiness her only concern.'' Netta's expression made it clear she considered herself that woman.

No doubt about it, the creature was touched in the upper story—perhaps even dangerous. Garth asked impatiently, ''Where is Serena now?''

''At the Crown and Scepter Inn in Aveton.''

His jaw dropped. ''What the devil is she doing there?''

Netta's face assumed a lugubrious expression that was belied by the slyness in her eyes.

''I fear that you can guess.''

His patience with this vexatious female was at an end. ''No, I cannot guess,'' he snapped. ''Which room?''

When she told him, he gave her a curt little bow. ''You must excuse me, Miss Bridger.''

''I have my carriage,'' she cried eagerly. ''I will take you.''

He raised his eyebrows. ''In a closed carriage?'' he queried. ''How very improper. Aren't you worried about your honor?''

She gave him a look that warned him *his* honor would more likely be in jeopardy in that carriage. He said curtly, ''I prefer horseback.''

As he turned to leave, Netta caught his arm. ''Please let me help you.''

''I do not see how you could,'' he said coldly, disengaging his arm from her determined grasp.

''You understand that Serena is not alone at the inn.''

''What she is doing there at all is beyond me, but I assume her maid is with her.''

''Not her maid—Lord Leland Caine!'' Netta tried to look funereal but her wily gray eyes betrayed her.

Garth, his patience and his politeness at an end,

glared at her. ''You little liar. What game are you playing?''

''It is Serena who has been playing games with you!
Where do you think she's been all these weeks?''

The weeks while she supposedly *had the measles!*
For a moment he could only stare incredulously into
Netta's crafty eyes. Then he rushed from the room
without a backward glance and down to the stable.

After Garth left Sally, she sent word to the stable that
as soon as the earl arrived home from London she
wanted two horses saddled for him and herself and
brought to the house.

Then she went up to Serena's room to change into
the blue habit with the gold frogging so that she would
be ready to leave for Tamar as soon as Thorley returned.

Sally was determined that Garth be told the truth as
quickly as possible. Although she cringed at the reper-
cussions that would surely follow, she would not deceive him any longer.

When Thorley arrived at the Abbey a half hour after
Garth's departure, Sally insisted upon talking to him
the moment he stepped across the threshold. She guided
him into the anteroom with the white plasterwork and
eggshell-blue walls.

Thorley looked shockingly haggard. His tired eyes
and the morose set of his face revealed that his mission
to London had not prospered.

When she told him of her promise to Garth, he said,
''It can wait until later today.''

''You said we would tell him as soon as you returned.''

''But I had hoped then to have the blunt to pay off
the loans,'' Thorley said. ''Both my banker and my
man of business say I have not a prayer of raising the
sum I need.''

Poor Thorley. Faced with having to go empty-handed
to Garth and tell him the truth, the earl's courage was

failing him. Sally didn't blame him. Her own was a little wobbly, too, but she had promised Garth that they would come to Tamar as soon as Thorley returned from London, and she intended to keep her word.

"We must go now," she said stubbornly, knowing it would be better to get it over with. The longer they deferred the confrontation, the more excuses Thorley would think of to continue to postpone it.

Thorley rubbed his face distractedly with his hands. "I cannot face Garth," he confessed. "I learned while I was in London that he paid for Serena's come-out season. I wondered why Papa didn't fly into the boughs over all those expensive gowns she bought. To think I called Garth a lick-penny to his face!"

Sally tried to cheer Thorley by telling him what Garth had said about forgiving the loans to escape an un-wanted marriage. "Perhaps he still will."

"Not when he learns how we have hoaxed him," the earl said gloomily.

"I have kept my promise to wait until you returned," she said, determined to tell Garth before they both lost their courage. "If you will not come with me now, I will go alone."

It was clear from Thorley's face that he did not be-lieve she would carry out her threat. He made no at-tempt to stop her as she strode purposefully to the door.

Outside, she mounted one of the two horses she had ordered brought up to the house and headed toward Tamar. Sally prayed that Thorley would follow her. She did not want to face Garth alone.

When she reached the great pile of cream stone that was Tamar, a groom waiting beside a closed carriage ran up to help her dismount. Clearly, Garth had visi-tors, and Sally was torn between vexation and cowardly relief that her confession to him would have to be post-poned until their departure.

As she went up the steps to the portico, a young woman attired in the first stare of fashion emerged from the house. A quick glance told Sally that the caller was no one she knew.

When they met on the steps, Sally would have continued past her had not the stranger shrieked and grabbed her arm.

"Serena, what are you doing here, you little fool!" The woman's nails bit painfully into Sally's arm, and her eyes were so full of fury that Sally instinctively recoiled from her.

"Why did you not do as I told you?" the stranger hissed. "You have ruined everything by coming here."

An appalling suspicion gripped Sally as to the stranger's identity and purpose, but she managed to ask innocently, "Have I now? Why is that?"

"Garth has just now left for the Crown and Scepter." The woman looked as though she would cheerfully murder Sally. "Why did you not stay there as I told you to do? It is crucial that Garth find you in Lee's embrace."

Except that Serena undoubtedly had not left the inn. Sally felt ill at the cruel scene she was certain would be enacted for Garth at the inn. It was guaranteed to ensure he broke his engagement.

The woman yanked on Sally's arm, trying to force her down the stairs. "Perhaps if we hurry, we can reach the inn before Garth . . ."

Sally pulled her arm from the woman's grasp. "Why is it crucial that Garth see me in Lee's arms?"

"How dare you begin to ask me questions now?" the woman exploded. "I know best, Serena! You know that."

"To the contrary, I am convinced that you do not," Sally said coldly, her irate gaze locking with Netta's.

"What has possessed you, Serena?" Netta asked, clearly shaken by this sudden contrariness. "You have been more than happy to do what I told you until now. Only remember, if it were not for me, you would never have been able to marry—" She broke off as a horse thundered up.

Netta turned white when she saw the rider. "Your brother! Do not say a word. Let me do the talking!"

Thorley dismounted from his lathered mount and started up the steps two at a time toward the women.

"Netta Bridger!" he exclaimed. "What the blazes are you doing here? Where is my sister?"

Netta stared wide-eyed at him, at Sally, then back at him as though he was dicked in the nob.

Sally ran down the stairs to her mare.

As she rode toward Aveton, she thought of Emma's suspicion that Netta had a *tendre* for Garth. Sally's hands clutched the reins convulsively as she divined the motive for Netta's conniving. The unscrupulous creature had turned Serena against her betrothed and now she had persuaded the ninnyhammer to take part in a cruel tableau at the Crown and Scepter for Garth's eyes. What better way to assure his undying enmity toward Serena than to have him find her in another man's arms?

Sally's only thought now was to try somehow to save Garth from the scene Netta had arranged for him, and she urged her mare to a gallop.

The sound of pounding hooves behind Sally told her that she was not alone on the road. Looking over her shoulder, she saw Thorley pushing his horse hard to catch up with her. She did not slow for him, but his faster mount soon closed the gap between them.

As he pulled alongside of her, he yelled, "Where are you going?"

Sally told him, and her reason for doing so.

His face turned ashen. "That is beyond the pale! How could Serena allow herself to be a party to such a heartless scheme? We must stop it. I know a shortcut that will get us to the inn ahead of him! Here is what we will do when we get there."

19

Garth galloped toward Aveton as though the hounds of hell were upon his heels. Had it not been for his aunt's letter telling him that London was abuzz with rumors about Serena and Lord Leland, he would have dismissed as nonsense Netta's claim that they were together at the Crown and Scepter.

Disconnected memories came together in his mind like pieces in a puzzle: the secrecy surrounding Serena's mysterious illness; her continuing reluctance to set a wedding date; the genuine surprise of both Emma and the Wycombe's butler when Serena had arrived with Thorley that first night Garth had seen her.

Weighing this evidence, he could find only one possible interpretation of it. Serena had eloped with Lord Leland. The Wycombes had succeeded in concealing her disappearance with a Banbury tale about the measles until the earl could find her.

Then, as luck would have it, Garth had been at Wycombe Abbey the night that Thorley returned with his runaway sister.

Garth did not know which infuriated him more: that he had been duped or that Serena had preferred that silly blockhead, Lord Leland, to himself. He could not deny that Lee was exceedingly handsome, but he would have thought that the cork-brain's slow wit and labored conversation would have quickly bored her.

Was that what had happened? Had she eloped with
Lord Leland, only to tire of him and come back home?

Or had it been money? Lee might be a duke's progeny, but he was the youngest of five sons. He would
never have more than a very modest income. Had Serena discovered she could not live in such straitened
circumstances and belatedly opted for her much wealth-
ier betrothed?

*"There is something we must discuss with you. We
will set the date then if it is what you still want."*

Yes, a little something to discuss: the trifling fact that
she had eloped with another man, although apparently
she had not married him.

Yet Garth could not doubt that her profession of love
for him that morning at Wycombe Abbey was genuine.
Had she, after her return home, fallen in love with him
as reluctantly as he had with her? But if that were the
case, why would she be with Lee at the Crown and
Scepter now? Or was she?

Garth, frantic to know the truth, reined his horse to
a stop outside the inn. As he rushed in, a bell on the
door announced his arrival. The cramped reception area
was empty.

He did not wait for someone to appear but dashed
up the stairs to the room where Netta had told him he
would find Serena.

The door apparently had not been securely latched
for as his fist banged upon it, it swung open.

There, before Garth's affronted eyes, was Serena,
wearing a filmy black negligee, locked in a passionate
embrace with Lord Leland Caine, clad only in his
breeches.

The sight of the sapskull making love to her was
more than Garth could endure.

As the door swung open, it hit a chair, and the lovers
started at the noise.

Lord Leland demanded, "How dare you burst in
upon us?"

"How dare *I?*" Garth cried. "What the devil are you doing with my betrothed?"

"She is my wife."

Until that moment, Garth had not comprehended how much he had come to love his sprite. His whole world seemed to explode and disintegrate in a fiery burst of rage. By God, he would kill this usurper!

Beyond rational thought, Garth ground out through clenched jaw, "She will be your widow! I am calling you out."

Lord Leland went white with fear, and he stepped hastily away from Serena. "But—but—you—you are said to be a crack shot," his lordship stammered.

Perhaps he was not as great a fool as Garth had thought.

"Yes," he acknowledged. "You should have considered that before you ran off with my betrothed. When were you married?"

"Six weeks ago."

Garth had thought they must have been shackled only that day. Instead Serena had been wed to Lee all the while she had been professing to want to marry him. Never before in his life had he felt like such a nodcock. Serena was the one that he ought to kill! The cruel, deceiving vixen!

He whirled on her. "You conniving piece of baggage. Why did you not tell me the truth this morning instead of contriving this scene? What did you think to gain by it?"

Serena stared blankly at him. For the first time since his return from Brazil, he saw the stupid dullness in her eyes that he detested, and that made him all the angrier.

She said nervously, "I do not know what you are talking about."

Even her voice had lost its flutelike timbre and taken on that whiny quality he had hated.

"You evil little witch, Serena! What did I ever do to you that made you want to humiliate me like this? I shall despise you till my dying day." He turned to Lord

Leland. "I will meet you at dawn tomorrow.. Until then."

His lordship, white with fear, said in a quavering voice, "Until dawn."

With a shriek, Serena threw herself at her husband. "No! No! You cannot meet him! He will kill you!"

Garth stalked out the door and down the stairs. Above him, Serena's shrieking grew more hysterical and less intelligible.

He vaulted into his saddle and galloped out of Aveton, so distraught that he did not even notice that he was riding in the opposite direction from Tamar.

He was about to turn back when he remembered that Lord Eldwin was visiting his sister and brother-in-law who lived down this road. Garth continued on. He would ask his friend to act as his second.

When she and Thorley rode up to the Crown and Scepter, Sally saw no sign of Garth's horse and breathed a sigh of relief. They must have reached the inn before him and would have time to put into action Thorley's hastily devised plan to discredit in Garth's eyes the scene that Netta had arranged.

Garth must be told the truth, but Sally would have done anything to spare him from learning it in the cruel manner that Netta had plotted.

Inside the inn, the reception area was empty, but far from quiet. The unintelligible screams of a woman in strong hysterics on the floor above were so loud that Sally had to raise her voice to be heard. "How shall we find the room your sister is in?"

"Easily," her brother said grimly. "You have only to follow the noise. I recognize Serena's shrieking."

He bounded up the steps two at a time. Sally ran after him, her hope that they had beaten Garth to the inn evaporating into foreboding. She prayed that some tragedy involving him and Lord Leland had not already occurred.

By the time she reached the room from which the

alarming screams were issuing, she had passed Thorley in her anxiety to see what had happened. The door to the room was partially open, and she looked in, half-expecting to see Garth lying wounded—or worse—upon the floor.

But there was no sign of him. The only male in the room, a bare-chested man, was trying unsuccessfully to quiet his hysterical companion whose back was to the door. Sally knew instantly from Emma's description that he was Lord Leland Caine.

The countess had been right when she had said he was more beautiful than handsome. He would have served as an ideal model for a sculpture of Adonis. Most women of Sally's acquaintance would have deeply envied his guinea-gold waves of hair over a noble brow, his long curling eyelashes and chiseled nose and cheekbones. Yet Sally felt no attraction to him. His face was too perfect. It lacked character, and his eyes had the dull look of a man whose understanding was inferior.

At the moment, his lordship appeared both beleaguered and helpless as he pleaded with the petite woman whose golden curls matched his own. "Now, now, my sweet, do not work yourself into such a state, I beg of you."

When he looked up and saw Thorley, the relief on his face was so intense it was comical.

"How excessively glad I am to see you, Wycombe. I pray you can calm your sister."

The hysterical woman whirled to look at the newcomers as Sally started to ask what was wrong. Her question died in her throat at the sight of the woman's face.

So, too, did Serena's screams when she saw Sally.

In the sudden quiet, the two women gaped at each other.

Serena's mouth formed an astonished O.

Sally was no less flabbergasted. Much as she had heard about the remarkable resemblance between herself and the earl's sister, not until this moment, when she observed it with her own eyes, was she able to appreciate how amazing it was.

Sally felt as though she was gazing into a looking glass at herself. Serena was truly her mirror image.

The silence was broken by Serena whispering wonderingly, "Sally?" She looked so stunned that it did not appear she was even consciously aware that she had spoken. Furthermore, she had uttered that single word so quietly that Sally was not certain that she had heard correctly. Surely, she could not have for there was no way that Serena could know her name.

"What did you say?" Sally demanded.

Serena did not answer.

Lord Leland goggled at Sally like a man seeing an apparition.

The condescending landlady, the one who had turned Sally away from the inn the night that she had arrived in Aveton, hurried into the room, drawn by the commotion. She must have just returned for she was still wearing a light-gray cape and a white bonnet that emphasized the boniness of her narrow face.

When the landlady recognized the earl, by far the most important personage in the Aveton area, her belligerent demeanor underwent a remarkable change.

"My lord," she simpered, dropping him a curtsy, "I am honored to have you visit my establishment. She looked at Sally standing beside him. "Is this your countess?"

"No, she is my sister, Lady Serena Keith."

That brought a startled ejaculation from Lord Leland, who was still gawking at Sally, and a shriek of outrage from the real Serena. "She is not! I am."

Thorley gave her a contemptuous perusal. "You are an impostor. That is why I am here. I heard that you were posing as my sister. I have come to warn you that if you continue to pretend to be her, I shall have you prosecuted."

Serena stamped her foot. "It is she who is the impostor," she screamed, pointing at Sally. "She is an actress named Sally Marlowe!"

So Sally had heard Serena right! But how could the earl's sister know her true identity? Both Sally and Thorley stared at Serena with such genuine astonishment that the landlady said sourly, "I see the truth of the matter in your faces."

Serena cried, "You see nothing of the sort, you meddling old harpy. Now leave us."

But this rude command had not the same effect upon the landlady now that her claim of ladyship was in doubt. The woman said coldly, "I don't take orders from the likes of you, you little hussy."

Serena gasped. Clearly no one had ever dared address her so disrespectfully before.

Thorley raked Serena with a look of contempt. "You will catch cold trying to persuade the world I do not know my own sister!"

"Aye, you will," the officious landlady interjected helpfully.

Lord Leland stared at his wife, a stupefied look upon his face. Sally saw real consternation in Serena's eyes as the precariousness of her position belatedly dawned on her. If Thorley were to insist that Sally, not Serena, was his sister, his word would carry. Serena would be a pariah, and her new husband would have grounds for an annulment of their marriage.

The proprietress pointed an accusing finger at his lordship. "This scoundrel passed himself off to me as Lord Leland Caine, the Duke of Hardcastle's son."

"That he is," the earl assured her, "and a suitor for my sister's hand."

The indignant landlady gestured toward Serena. "He told me she was his wife! Who is she?"

Thorley said calmly, "She has betrayed her identity to us. She is an actress named Sally Marlowe who I understand is part of a band of strolling players."

The proprietress, clearly outraged that such riffraff had desecrated her respectable premises, demanded,

"And the other woman who is traveling with this pair? Who might she be?"

"Another actress from the same troupe," Thorley said carelessly, ensuring that Netta Bridger would receive an uncomfortable, but well-deserved surprise when she returned.

"It pains me to say that Lord Leland came here today intent upon using this actress to trick me into giving him the permission I earlier denied him to marry my sister."

Lord Leland had the dazed look of a man who had been floored by a facer.

The landlady, looking as bewildered as his lordship, gasped. "Trick you, milord? How?"

"You apprehend the remarkable resemblance between his companion and my sister. He planned that I should discover him in a compromising position with her here and, thinking her my sister, agree to the marriage. Fortunately, he wrote my sister of his plan, and she wisely wanted no part of such a disgraceful strategy." Thorley smiled lovingly at Sally. "Instead, she came to me and told me the truth."

"Yes, I did," Sally chimed in, looking at Lord Leland with contrite eyes. "I am sorry, Lee, but I had to tell Thor. I could never be party to such a ramshackle scheme as that." Her voice was thick with reproach. "I cannot conceive how you could think that I would."

Lord Leland's eyes appeared to be starting from his noble head. His tongue, never quick under the best of circumstances, seemed to tie itself in knots. "But I didn't . . . Thought . . . didn't write . . . she said . . ."

Sally offered up a prayer of thanks that his lordship was as great a noddy as everyone said.

Serena, her face as white as winter snow, gave her husband a frightened look.

Sally could not help but feel sorry for her, even though she had helped bring this unhappy situation upon herself. At least, Garth would now be spared the pain of seeing the cruel scene that Serena and Netta had arranged for him.

Or had he been spared?

Sally edged nervously toward the window and looked out. There was still no sign of him. Surely, it could not have taken him this long to reach the inn. A horrible suspicion began to dawn on Sally and she asked Lord Leland bluntly, "Has Sir Garth Taymor been here?"

He nodded glumly. "Never seen a man in such a rage."

She and Thorley exchanged dismayed glances. Their little charade had been in vain. All they could hope to accomplish now was to avoid as much scandal as possible.

Switching tactics abruptly, Sally said to Lord Leland, "I wish you had not come here like this, darling. I finally managed to persuade my brother that we truly love each other, and he said he would permit us to marry after all. I pray that this crack-brained escapade of yours has not closed his mind against you."

His lordship looked like a man who had unknowingly stumbled into a ward at Bedlam and was now trapped among its mad inmates.

Sally turned to the earl. "Please, I beg of you, Thorley, forgive Lee, and give us your blessing."

The earl appeared to consider her plea gravely. He said at last, "Yes, Serena, I will, for I know how men stymied in love often do desperate things."

Sally gave Lord Leland an adoring look. "Oh, darling, we shall be so happy together."

His lordship, utterly befuddled, sank down upon the bed as though his handsome legs were no longer capable of supporting him.

Thorley turned to the landlady. "Now if you will excuse us, madam. I trust that no word of what passed here today will be heard outside this room. If any hint of this leaks out . . ." Threat was implicit in his voice as he let it trail off ominously.

It was not lost upon the landlady who hastened to

swear that the good Lord might strike her dead if a word should ever pass her lips about what had occurred.

Sally suspected the overbearing woman might even keep her oath, if only to hide the scandalous fact that, despite her vigilance, her premises had been debauched by the presence of an actress.

As the door closed behind her stiff figure, Serena grabbed Thorley's arm. "You knew all along, didn't you? You pretended to be ignorant of what Papa and I argued about, but he told you!"

Thorley stared at her as though she were touched in the upper works. "Told me what? Clearly you know a great deal that I do not. What are you talking about?"

Serena stared sullenly down at the floor. "Nothing."

"Then I hope you enjoy your life as Sally Marlowe," Thorley said coldly. "I collect, Lee, that felicitations are in order. I wish you happy on your marriage to this *actress.*"

"But I am Serena!" she protested, beginning to cry. "You have to believe me, Lee."

She threw herself upon her husband, still seated on the bed in a state of profound shock, rousing him from his stupor. He hugged her tightly to him, then looked defiantly up at his two visitors.

"Don't pretend to understand what's going on here, but I know the woman I married. This is she, and I love her."

His lordship's understanding might not be swift, but he was a good and faithful man. Sally hoped Serena appreciated that.

Apparently she did, for she clung to him, her face against his bare chest. A muffled plea rose from her lips. "Promise me, Lee, you will not desert me, no matter what they say about me."

"I promise," he reassured her.

For a moment, they held each other in silence.

Then a frown marred his lordship's perfect brow. "But I tell you, my love, that you will have nothing

more to do with Netta Bridger,'' he said with a stern-
ness that surprised Sally.

It apparently surprised his wife as well, for Serena
said falteringly, "But if it were not for Netta—"

"If it were not for her," he interrupted bitterly, "I
would not be fighting a duel tomorrow. Never did understand why we had to run this queer rig of hers.
Warned you no good would come of it. Warned you
that Sir Garth would likely call me out, but you wouldn't
listen, and now he has.''

That threatened to send Serena into another bout of
hysteria.

"You cannot meet him," she cried, beginning to sob.
"Promise me, you will not."

"Must, love," he said stubbornly. "Not such a cod's
head I don't know that honor requires it."

Men and their foolish ideas of honor, Sally thought
grimly. She would have to find a way to put a stop to
the duel.

She turned to Thorley. "Come, we must locate Garth
and make him understand that his quarrel is not with
poor Lord Leland but with us."

"Then," Thorley predicted glumly, "he will call me
out, too."

When Sally and the earl reached Tamar, Garth was
not there. They waited for more than an hour, but still
he did not appear. On the slim possibility that he might
be waiting for them at Wycombe Abbey, they went
home, but he was not there either.

The dinner hour passed, and night fell, but still nothing was heard from Garth. By then Sally was so consumed with worry over him that Thorley took her back
to Tamar.

This time Garth was home, but his butler coldly informed them that his master would not see anyone from
Wycombe Abbey.

Sally, thrusting her chin up at a stubborn angle, announced, "He will see me! I shall not leave until he does. Tell him so."

The butler, awed by her determination, went down the hall into the breakfast parlor that Garth had turned into his informal dining room and shut the door.

It remained closed for what seemed like an eternity to her. When at last it reopened, the butler emerged with a second man behind him. Sally's heart sank when she saw that he was not Garth, but Lord Eldwin Drake. She remembered Emma telling her that he had returned to the neighborhood to visit his sister.

Lord Eldwin regarded her and Thorley with revulsion. "I cannot believe, Lady *Caine*, that you could be so brass-faced as to show yourself here after what you have done. Don't mind telling you that I think you a cruel, contemptible creature. Could you not have told Garth the truth instead of staging that unconscionable scene at the Crown and Scepter?"

Sally ignored his censure. "I must talk to Garth."

"Won't see you. Swears he never wants to lay eyes on you again."

"I will not leave until I see him!" she persisted.

"Not to wrap it in clean linen, he's in no shape to see you or anyone," Eldwin said. "Properly shot in the neck, he is. Most understandable after what you did to him today."

He turned his ire on Thorley. "As for you, Wycombe, I never thought that you would lend yourself to such a shabby trick. I am glad, though, you are here. It saves me a trip to Wycombe Abbey tonight. I am Garth's second for tomorrow's duel, and I presume that you will act in the same capacity for your new brother-in-law. Don't mind telling you I don't approve of dueling. But Garth insists there must be a meeting at dawn."

"Yes, there will be." Sally said, a plan taking shape in her mind.

Lord Eldwin asked contemptuously, "Does it please you to have two men dueling over you? Don't mind telling you, Serena, that Garth deserved so much better than you! You led him on, pretended you wanted to marry him, even told him that you loved him when, all the while, you were married to another. Have you no shame?''

"Aye, Oi do, but Oi ain't yer bloody Lady Serena," Sally said in the same shrill tone that she had employed that day by the Walcott players' tent.

"The actress?" his lordship exclaimed, nonplussed. Then his eyes narrowed suspiciously. "Or was it you all the time, Serena? Did you play me for a fool that day?"

"No, I did not. I am who I said I was. If you are truly Garth's friend, Lord Eldwin, you will help me for his sake."

20

Early the next morning, darkness was giving way to the first gray of an overcast dawn, as Garth drove his curricle toward the meadow that had been chosen for his duel with Leland Caine. Waves of mist rolled intermittently over the land like malevolent ghosts on the prowl. The perfect backdrop, Garth though wearily, for what was about to occur.

No groom accompanied him for his clandestine meeting with Lee. Only Lord Eldwin was with Garth, and the two men did not speak. On the seat between them lay a walnut case decorated with silver filigree that contained Garth's dueling pistols, a pair of Manton's finest.

Garth's fury at Serena had been too fiery and all-consuming to sustain itself. Now it had burned itself out, leaving only ashes and bleak despair in his heart.

He should hate her.

He did hate her!

But even as he assured himself of that, he knew in the depths of his contrary heart that he still cared for her.

When he thought of what his life at Tamar would be like without his sprite, of the endless, lonely years stretching ahead of him, of never holding her in his arms again, of never making love to her, he did not care whether he died in the duel that morn.

Nor did he particularly want to kill her husband—except when he thought of Lee making love to Serena. Then he gnashed his teeth in jealous rage and there was murder in his heart. He suspected that the poor nodcock had been as much a victim of Serena's manipulations as he had. And of Netta's. Garth was convinced that devious female had played a crucial role in his mortification.

He glanced over at Eldwin. At first, his friend had argued passionately against the duel, insisting that Serena was not worth fighting over. Then, after Wycombe and his sister had come to Tamar last night, Eldwin had been uncharacteristically silent, saying only that arrangements for the duel had been completed and Garth must try to get some sleep before the dawn meeting.

Of course, that had been impossible. Garth had been too tormented by thoughts of Serena's terrible treachery to catch more than a few restless minutes of sleep. He cringed in shame. How could he have been so stupid and gullible that he had believed the lying jezebel when she told him she loved him? Even as she was doing so, she was plotting that humiliating scene at the Crown and Scepter. God, but her cruelty and duplicity sickened him.

He hated her! Lee was welcome to her!

Garth turned into the meadow. Through the gray light and rolling mist, he saw Wycombe's closed carriage beside a large oak at the far end of the meadow. The earl stood alone beside it. Neither Lord Leland Caine nor the surgeon that Eldwin said Thorley would bring were visible.

Garth stopped his curricle beside the carriage. Jumping down, he asked, "Is my opponent here, Wycombe?"

"Yes, both your opponent and Serena are here," Thorley said with a sweep of his hand toward the rear of his carriage. Two figures in tandem, the first in skirts, the second in breeches, emerged from behind it and moved through the mist toward Garth.

Despite his rage at Serena, his heart leaped at the sight of her walking toward him in an elaborate red carriage gown and matching wool redingote trimmed with jet buttons.

He had told himself that he never wanted to set eyes on the vicious, perfidious harpy again so long as he lived.

But now he could not tear his gaze from that beautiful face, could not even spare so much as a glance for his opponent walking behind her.

Garth had not expected Serena to come this morning. Did the lying little witch hope to witness her husband dispose of him once and for all? A fresh wave of rage washed over him. If she had come to watch him die, she would be disappointed.

Until he saw her, Garth had planned to waste his ball harmlessly in the air, but now he would not do so. He was a crack shot, and he would not give Serena the satisfaction of seeing him spare Lord Leland.

As she approached Garth, the spirited vitality that had captivated him the past month seemed to have been drained from her. Her eyes were so dull that he felt an involuntary pang of concern. Was she worried at what her inept husband's fate would be at Garth's hands? Well she ought to be.

He ruthlessly crushed his flicker of sympathy for her, reminding himself that she had shown him no mercy the previous day and that he despised her for her evil, rotten trickery.

Her gaze met his only briefly, then skidded quickly away toward the ground.

"I would not be able to look me in the eye either, Serena," he said scathingly, "after all the lies you have told me, you evil, heartless jade.

"As for you . . ." He tore his gaze away from Serena long enough to look for the first time at the figure behind her.

It flashed through Garth's tormented brain that he was well and truly losing his mind.

It was not Lord Leland that he saw there in the ghostly mist, but his sprite in the blue riding coat with the gold frogging and those outrageous breeches.

Her brilliant blue eyes did not evade his gaze as Serena's had done, but met it with a look of such love that he suddenly felt as though he could not breathe.

He groaned and ran his hand over his eyes to banish this apparition, but when he removed his hand, it was still there.

Garth stared incredulously at the two figures standing before him. They were identical in face and form. Only their clothes were different.

No, not truly identical. Even without the breeches, Garth could tell which was his sprite by the aura of vitality that crackled around her and the way her eyes met his squarely.

Comprehension struck him like a sneak blow from behind. No wonder she had looked so stricken when he had said it was as though she were a different woman from the one he had known two years ago.

Damn her, she *was* a different woman!

A hot flush of mortification and rage rose in his face as he began to grasp the dimensions and ramifications of the hoax that had been played on him.

A collage of images flashed through Garth's memory: the sprite darting about examining the columbine, studying the leaves of the laburnum tree, raising her face to welcome the spray of the cascade, challenging him, riding astride in her breeches, swimming in the pond.

Not one of those things would that timid, indolent shatterbrain Serena have done. He should have known that. He fiercely castigated himself for his own stupidity. So much that had mystified him about her suddenly made sense.

What did not make sense to him was why this heartless sham had been perpetrated on him. He could not conceive why anyone would go to the trouble to devise

such an elaborate and vicious charade except to hold
someone they utterly despised up to ridicule.

"Who the devil are you?" he demanded harshly.
"And where is my opponent?"

"I am your opponent," she replied. "Your quarrel
is with me, not Lord Leland, who is as innocent as you
in this wretched deception. I am the one who deceived
you. I am the one you should want to kill."

"I may do so yet," he said through clenched jaw.
"Who are you?"

"My name is Sally Marlowe."

"Where did you find her?" he demanded of Thorley,
who was eyeing him uneasily.

"In Aveton. I, too, thought she was my sister, and I
took her up into my curricle. She is an actress."

"You hardly need tell me that! A very talented actress, I'll grant that." A recollection tugged at his
memory, and he whirled on Lord Eldwin. "Could this
be the strolling player you saw, the one you said looked
like Serena?" At the time, Garth had dismissed what
his drunken friend had said about the performer's resemblance to his betrothed as bosky rambling.

Eldwin nodded affirmatively.

So Thorley had hired an actress to impersonate his
sister to her betrothed. Suddenly, Garth thought he
comprehended the reason for such an unspeakable
fraud. It so sickened and enraged him that for a moment, until the blinding wave of black fury that washed
over him receded, he could not even speak.

Then he turned savagely on Thorley. "So I was good
enough to borrow money from, but not good enough
to marry your sister."

"I never thought that!" the earl cried in shocked
accents. "I—"

"Don't lie to me anymore, Thorley, or so help me I
will call you out, too! To save your sister for a higher-
born husband and still escape repaying your father's
loans, you hit upon substituting an actress you picked
off the streets." A muscle in Garth's jaw twitched con-

vulsively. "What enormous amusement you must have derived from the prospect of marrying me, wholly unsuspectingly, off to such a lowborn creature! I never realized how cruelly malicious you are."

Thorley, looking aghast, protested, "It was never our intention to do anything other than to get you to cry off."

"As if I could believe anything you said," Garth cried contemptuously, in the throes of a fury so intense he was shaking.

He had always thought himself a knowing one, awake on every suit, but his deceivers had perceived him as the flattest of the flats, to be easily gulled, and he had proved them right.

His heart had already been grievously wounded. This new realization shredded his pride, too. He whirled on the impostor who had made such a fool of him.

She visibly blanched at the rage in his eyes.

"And you, you lying little witch. I need not ask why you agreed to it. Suddenly you would be lifted from the gutter into a luxurious life among the *ton* that you can never hope to attain except by deception."

His sense of having been most cruelly, abominably, and humiliatingly used was feeding on itself so voraciously that by now he scarcely knew what he was saying. "No doubt you hoped to make me so besotted over you that by the time I learned the truth I would no longer care what you were."

Tears glistened in Sally's eyes.

"How long after we were married would it have been before you told me the truth? When you were increasing with our first child? No, more likely you planned to wait until after it was born!"

A single tear coursed down her cheek. "I would not have married you under false pretenses."

"Would you not have, you lying jade?" he jeered. "Then why did you try so hard to make me think you loved me?"

Her gaze met his unwaveringly. "Because I do love

you. That was why I refused to set a wedding date until you knew the truth."

He snorted in furious disbelief. "Next you'll tell me that cows fly."

"Garth, listen to me," she pleaded. "I am the same woman I was yesterday when you were so anxious to marry me. Yet now that you know I have not a title before my name, you will have none of me. It is not I who am different, only your perception of me."

He was too mortified and bitterly wounded at her having played him for such a witless Johnny Raw to heed what she said. "Yes," he snapped, "now I know you for the evil, deceitful doxy you are!"

Abruptly, he turned on his heel and bounded into his curricle. Lord Eldwin, seeing the look on his friend's face, hastily followed him.

When Garth had taken up the reins of his matched pair, he glared down at Thorley. "By God, to think I counted you as a friend. How could you do this to me?"

The earl had the grace to look stricken. "I dared not tell you Serena had run away rather than marry you because I could not pay off my father's loans."

"Have I ever been less than generous with you, Thorley? Had you come to me and told me the truth, I would have forgiven the loans. But now, after this shameless deception, I shall demand repayment of every shilling."

He glared down at Sally with hate-filled eyes. "I collect you were part of that troupe I saw perform *Antony and Cleopatra*. How unfortunate for me that you were not in the cast that day."

"But I was."

"I did not see you."

"Yes, you did—both before the play, and in it," she said quietly. "I was Cleopatra."

He could only stare at her, bereft of speech. Surely she could not have been the fiery black-haired actress to whom he had been so attracted! He could not believe it. Then he remembered the times when Serena—or whatever the devil her name was—had reminded him of her. At last, he understood why.

When he recovered his voice, he said with scorching sarcasm, "Let me congratulate you again on your enormous talent. You are such a consummate actress that you even had me believing that you loved me."

She met his infuriated gaze without flinching. "I swear to you I do love you."

"And you proved it by deceiving and playing me for a fool! If that is the way you treat a man you profess to love, I am grateful that you did not consider me your enemy."

His gaze, filled with loathing, swept her slowly from head to foot. This time, he noticed with satisfaction, she did flinch. He had never seen such tormented eyes as hers. But the ungovernable fury that possessed him stifled any sympathy for her. Instead he barked, "As for me, I shall despise you until my dying day."

He cracked his whip over his horses, and the curricle departed in a cloud of dust.

21

As Garth's curricle raced away from the meadow, Sally's heart crumpled in despair. Her audacious gamble had failed.

The revulsion she had seen in Garth's eyes when he looked at her would haunt her all the rest of her days.

She could not blame him for hating her, especially when he mistakenly believed that her goal had been to dupe him into a misalliance. It had never occurred to her he would think such a hideous thing. But he did.

Nothing would convince him now that she loved only him, and not his wealth or social position.

But even if he had believed her, he was far too proud a man to marry a strolling player. Thorley had been right. Garth would have nothing to do with a woman from the depths of society. She should have known that. After all, it was her indignation over his pride that had spurred her into this disastrous charade in the first place. She had wanted to punish him for his toploftiness.

She had succeeded in ways he never deserved and she never intended.

And in the end, the person punished most was herself. She had not only lost the one man she had ever loved, but she had made him despise her in the bargain.

Sadly, Sally went around the carriage, using it to conceal her while she put on the skirt of the blue riding habit over her breeches.

By the time she was finished, Thorley had bundled himself in the many-caped gray coat he had temporarily filched from his still-sleeping coachman. Like Garth, he had brought no servants with him to witness what transpired in the meadow that dawn.

The door of the carriage was open. Serena had joined her husband, who had been concealed inside the equipage during the confrontation with Garth. Sally climbed inside, too, and sat on the seat opposite them.

The events of the past day had had a maturing effect upon his lordship. He had begun to act with more assurance and authority. Serena, clearly awed by this display of masculine dominance, had acquiesced to his order that she have nothing more to do with that "infernal Netta."

After all, it was Netta's conniving that had set in motion this whole unhappy chain of events. She had convinced the gullible Serena that if she did not flee her brother's house and elope with Lee, Thorley would keep her a prisoner until he could force her to marry Garth. Then the two females between them had managed to persuade a dubious Lord Leland of it.

Netta, after acrimonious confrontations the previous day with both Lord Leland and the Crown and Scepter's landlady, had retreated to London.

Serena had reluctantly gone along with Sally's plan for stopping the duel only because she was desperate to protect her husband.

She still steadfastly refused to divulge how it was that she knew Sally's identity. Her terror whenever she was questioned about it was unmistakable, and no amount of threatening and cajoling loosened her tongue.

Thorley mounted the box and headed his carriage back toward the road. As he turned on to it, an early-morning stage rattled by, traveling in the opposite direction. Thorley pulled his hat lower over his forehead, even though it was highly unlikely anyone riding on a common stage would recognize the Earl of Wycombe.

Inside the carriage, Sally looked enviously at Serena

on the opposite seat, nestled in the protection of her husband's arm. Sally longed for nothing so much as Garth's arm about her, but she knew with bleak certainty that she would never feel his touch again.

She stared miserably out the window. If only she had never agreed to hoax Garth. If . . . if . . . if . . .

The road forked and the coach took the branch to the right. Two women trudged wearily along the side of it. Both were wrapped in cloaks to ward off the early-morning chill. One carried a worn portmanteau, and Sally surmised that they must have been set down from the stage at the point where the road divided.

Something about the way they walked and the worn bag that the younger carried caught Sally's attention. She banged against the carriage roof for Thorley to stop. By the time he was able to do so, they were a hundred feet beyond the women.

Sally flung open the carriage door, gathered up the voluminous blue skirt of the riding habit, jumped out, and ran back down the road to the women.

"Mama, Mama," she cried, throwing herself into the arms that opened to receive her.

The two women hugged fiercely. Then Sally embraced the other woman, her married sister Ann. The resemblance between them was strong, even though Ann was taller and plumper.

"Why have you come here, Mama?" Sally asked, looking lovingly into her mother's face that, before age and illness had taken its toll, had been very like her own. "I would not have thought your health would permit it."

"I pray it will not be the death of her," Ann said fervently, "but she would not be dissuaded from coming after she received your letter. It so agitated her that she insisted upon setting out at once."

"I am surprised Papa permitted it."

"He did not know." Ann cast a frightened glance at her mother. "Mama would not let me tell him we were going. Indeed, she refuses to tell even me why we have come.''

"Will you tell me, Mama?" Sally asked gently.

Tears welled in the tired, faded eyes that once had been as bright a blue as her daughter's. "I should think you would know why by now."

Her gaze moved from Sally's puzzled face toward the stopped carriage.

Sally glanced back over her shoulder. Thorley had scrambled down from the box and was helping his sister out of the equipage. Her indolent husband apparently had elected to remain in the coach.

Mama gasped as she saw the girl coming toward them in a handsome red wool redingote trimmed with jet buttons. A look of pure joy transformed the older woman's worn face.

"Serena," she murmured, a sob in her voice.

But if Mama was happy to see Serena, the feeling was clearly not reciprocated. The hatred in the girl's eyes as she looked at Mrs. Marlowe stunned Sally.

Ann asked, "Who is this girl?"

"Lady Serena Keith," Sally answered. "We look enough alike to be twins, do we not?"

Serena glared at Sally and her mother for a long moment before saying in a voice of ice, "We *are* twins."

Mama turned her face into Sally's shoulder and began to sob.

Thorley, Sally, and Ann stared at Serena, speechless with shock.

Sally, who was stroking her mother's hair in a vain attempt to comfort her, was the first to recover her voice. "Is it true, Mama?" she asked gently.

"Yes," her mother sobbed.

Thorley said in a strangled voice, "How can that be? I don't understand."

Serena whirled on him. "So Papa did not tell you the truth!"

"Dammit, Serena, explain what this is all about!"

But she remained mulishly silent.

Sally guessed at least some of the story. "So, Mama," she said, still hugging her weeping parent to her, "that is why you came when you learned I was at Wycombe Abbey. You knew that I would surely meet my twin. You must tell us the story since Serena is not inclined to do so."

Between bitter sobs, Mama told of that cold, cruel winter in Yorkshire when her twins had been born. She and her husband had been left penniless and stranded in the North Riding when their company of strolling players had fallen on hard times and disbanded.

Thorley's parents were also living there at the time. Even then, Thorley's father, not yet the Earl of Wycombe but still Viscount Keith, had lived beyond his means. As punishment, his irate father had exiled him and his family to a remote estate in the North Riding.

Thorley's kindly mother had taken pity on the Marlowes. She had hired Mrs. Marlowe, hugely pregnant with twins, as her companion and given her husband and three children shelter.

"Had it not been for her, we would all have starved," Mrs. Marlowe recalled tearfully.

She and Lady Wycombe, perhaps in part because both were breeding and expected to be confined at about the same time, grew very fond of each other.

Thorley's mother went into labor first, producing a frail, undersized daughter. It was a long and difficult birth that left her unable to bear more children. She was distraught at this news, and it was feared that if her baby did not survive, her mind would become unhinged.

Mrs. Marlowe said sadly, "Unfortunately, the infant died two days later while I was being delivered of twin daughters." She turned to Thorley. "Your mama was never told of her death. Your papa persuaded us that after all your mama had done for us the least we could do was allow one of our twins to be substituted for the dead infant. Poor Lady Wycombe was too sick to see her babe for more than an instant when it was born so she never suspected the switch.''

Thorley exclaimed, ''Good God, are you telling me Mama never knew that Serena was not her own daughter?''

''It was all the earl's idea,'' Mrs. Marlowe explained. ''He was so worried about your mama. Whatever his other faults, and I know he was a shocking spendthrift, he adored her. He would have done anything for her. Only he, the nurse, my husband, and I knew of the switch. Everyone else was told that the dead babe was one of our twins.''

For a moment, no one spoke, then Sally turned to Serena. ''Lord Wycombe told you the truth about your birth during that terrible fight you had with him, didn't he?''

Serena did not deny it. Instead she said bitterly, ''I told him that I would not marry Garth. Netta had convinced me that the son of a money-grubbing baronet was beneath me. Papa pointed out all the advantages of the marriage, but I swore to him that nothing could force me to go through with it.''

Serena shuddered visibly. ''I have never seen him so angry. He shouted at me that it was I who was beneath Garth, that he was my only hope for anything approaching a respectable marriage. Then he told me who I really was.''

Her voice broke, and it was a moment before she could continue. ''I had always suspected the way Papa ignored me that he did not love me, but it was worse than that. He told me he hated the sight of me because I was an impostor without an ounce of his own blood in me. He called me rubbish dredged from the gutter and promised that he would toss me back into it if I did not marry Garth as he wanted. Now that Ma—his wife—was dead, he did not care what happened to me.''

A red flush of humiliation stained Serena's cheeks. ''He swore that he would never permit me, the spawn of lowly strolling players, to marry into a noble family and dilute their precious bloodlines. That was why he had been so happy to sell me to Garth's father. He did not want to pawn off inferior goods on his aristocratic friends, but he despised Sir Malcolm. He told me about the loans and congratulated himself on being so clever as to foist me off upon that parvenu at a handsome profit.''

Tears were pouring down Serena's cheeks now like rain-swollen rivulets. ''If I cried off, he would tell the world the truth about me, and I would be ostracized by society. He taunted me that the only reason anyone would marry me was because I was thought to be his daughter. When the truth was known, no man of the *ton* would have such an insipid ninnyhammer as me.''

''So you were determined to prove that he was wrong,'' Sally guessed. ''You set your cap for a duke's son.''

Her twin nodded miserably. ''Not only was Lee the Duke of Hardcastle's son, but he was so handsome—a husband to be proud of. But then I fell in love with him,'' she wailed. ''When he learns the truth, he will want nothing more to do with me, and I love him so desperately.''

Sally understood Serena's pain and despair all too well. She, too, had deceived the man she loved and lost him.

Serena suddenly turned on her mother with such savage fury in her eyes that the older woman instinctively drew back. ''How could you have blithely sold me, your own flesh and blood, to be raised by strangers who did not love me?''

Thorley cried, ''That's not true, Serena! Mama adored you! There was nothing she would not have done for you.''

''Only because she thought I was her daughter! Had she known the truth, she would have hated me as much as your papa did.''

Serena's anguish tore at Sally's heart. Now she understood what had caused her twin to change so much the past year. She had been raised as a proud, pampered lady, spoiled and cosseted. Then Serena, so proud of her high birth, had been brutally informed that she was far less than she thought herself. Worse, the man she had loved as her father told her that he despised her. She was untrained and unfit for any occupation other than a nobleman's wife. But there could be no hope of that if the truth about her was revealed.

She lived in terror that if the secret of her birth became known, she would find herself utterly alone, unloved and unwanted, cast out into a hostile world that she was totally unequipped to deal with.

In her panic and her bitterness, Serena had turned hateful toward the members of her putative family because she was convinced they would hate and ostracize her if they knew what she really was.

Serena desperately needed to be loved for herself. Sally understood that so well. It was what she had hoped in vain Garth would be able to do.

Thorley stepped forward and put his arm comfortingly around Serena. "Papa was in his cups that day you argued. You know that he was prone to say wild and cruel things that he did not mean when he was like that."

"Oh, he meant every word," Serena retorted with a despairing, futile brush at the tears on her cheek.

Thorley asked, "Could you not have trusted me enough to tell me the truth?"

"Why, so you could send me packing?" she countered bitterly. "I dared tell no one the truth, not even Netta. I knew if I told you, you would have nothing more to do with me."

Thorley gently brushed the tears from Serena's cheeks. "Poppet, you *are* my sister. You always will be."

Her eyes widened at his loving use of his childhood endearment for her. "You have not called me that for a long time, Thor."

"Because I have been so exasperated with you. I

could not understand why you were behaving as you were. Now I do.''

He held her tightly to him, and she clung to him, sobbing into his many-caped gray coat.

''My poor poppet,'' he murmured, stroking her blonde curls comfortingly.

''Oh, Thor,'' she cried, ''I am so afraid that Lee will have our marriage annulled.''

Sally's heart went out to her weeping sister. Would Lee abandon Serena, as Garth had Sally, when he found out the truth about her birth?

''I think, poppet, that you do your husband as much an injustice as you did me. Does she, Lee?''

Sally turned and saw that his lordship at some point had gotten out of the carriage and was standing a little away from them, a silent, unnoticed observer to the scene.

Lord Leland said nothing, only held out his arms to his wife, and she ran into them.

Sally studied the newlyweds clinging to each other. Serena was lucky. A prouder or more ambitious man might not have been so accepting.

Emma had been right: they were well matched both in temperament and intellect. Lord Leland would have bored Sally to distraction, just as Serena would have bored Garth, but she suspected that they would be happy together.

The new Lady Caine asked her husband brokenly, ''What will your papa say when he learns the truth of me?''

His lordship's newfound maturity faltered a little. He answered nervously, ''Papa will not like it.''

''Papa need never know,'' Thorley assured him. ''Serena is my sister.'' He smiled at her, then glanced toward Sally. ''I only wish that I could make her twin my sister, too.''

Serena stepped out of the protection of her husband's arms and confronted her mother. ''Why did you not want me?'' She gestured at Sally. ''Why did you choose to keep her instead of me?''

''My dearest child,'' Mrs. Marlowe said sadly. She tried to embrace her daughter, but Serena angrily pushed her away.

''Not dear enough for you to keep me!''

''Now listen to me, Serena,'' Mrs. Marlowe said, suddenly speaking in the voice that had once riveted audiences. ''We did not give you away because we did not want you! We did it because we believed it was the very best thing that we could do for you. I wanted nothing more than to keep you. Not a day of my life has passed without my thinking of you a dozen times. And when death took two of my other children from me, I wondered if that was God's way of punishing me for giving you up. But I did so for the best of reasons.''

''Yes, money!'' Serena said bitterly. ''Papa—the earl—told me he paid my real father a great deal of money for me.''

''Yes, he did,'' Mrs. Marlowe acknowledged, ''but I did not learn about it until years later.'' She turned to her other two daughters. ''That is how Papa got the money to buy the theater in Harrogate.''

Serena said caustically, ''You sold me for thirty pieces of silver!''

''The money, which I did not even know about, had nothing to do with my decision to part with you,'' Mrs. Marlowe said.

Seeing the disbelief in Serena's eyes, her mother began pacing in an agitated little circle. ''How can I make you understand how it was for us then? We had no money, no food. Had it not been for Lady Wycombe's kindness, we would all have starved that winter. We chose to give you up instead of your sister because it was obvious from the start that you were the smaller and more delicate twin, and would be less able to survive the rigors of our life.''

Mrs. Marlowe stopped pacing and faced her unhappy daughter again. ''I think every mother wants the best she can provide for her child. Your papa and I were too poor even to feed you properly, and I knew dear Lady Wycombe would take excellent care of you. Indeed, your papa and I both looked upon it as a chance of a lifetime for you. How could we deny you the opportunity for a cosseted, privileged life of wealth and leisure? It would have been cruel to do so.''

Mama looked beseechingly at Serena. ''My dearest child, it was you, not Sally, that I considered the lucky one. I gave you up because I loved you so much that I wanted you to have the very best life possible!''

Serena's eyes brightened. She threw her arms around her mother, and they hugged each other.

22

Sally stood in the wings of the cavernous Drury Lane Theater, awaiting her cue for her debut on the London stage, the zenith of every British actress's ambition.

She had Emma to thank for being here. Through friends, the countess had arranged an audition for Sally, and she had done so well that she was given probationary status with the company. She had expected her first performance before a real London audience to come in a minor role, but fate had intervened.

The popular actress who was to play Juliet tonight had lost her voice to a severe chest cold, and her understudy was in Watford at the bedside of her dying mother. Sally had so impressed the theater's manager with her talent that he drafted her into emergency service. She was thrilled and awed that she would be making her London debut in a starring role.

And terribly nervous. Indeed, Sally was surprised at how jittery she was even though she had played Juliet numerous times.

But never at Drury Lane before critical, sophisticated Londoners. In vain did she try to quiet her anxiety by telling herself it was just another audience. But she knew better. Her whole future hinged on the response of this one.

Her apprehension had not been eased by the hissing

among the audience when it was announced before the
play began that Sally Marlowe, an unknown, would be
substituting for the noted actress who had been scheduled to play Juliet.

Sally had dreamed so often of standing on this very
spot. Yet now that she actually was, her thrill at reaching it was sadly diminished by thoughts of Garth.

He, too, was in London. Had been all these weeks
since the aborted duel. He had left Tamar that same
morning.

Happily, a scandal had been avoided. Thorley had
visited Netta Bridger in London. He never divulged
what methods he employed to induce her to remain silent on all matters pertaining to the affair, but he succeeded.

The inevitable rumors made the rounds, but Lord
Rudolph Oldfield, the *ton*'s most malicious gossip, pronounced that no credence should be placed in them and
they had faded away.

Garth, as he had promised he would, was demanding
immediate repayment of the Wycombes' loans, and the
young earl faced ruin.

Thorley sent an announcement, purposely vague in
the details, to the London papers that Serena had been
married privately to Lord Leland. The newlyweds were
now living quietly on a small Bedfordshire estate owned
by Lee's father.

Thorley's announcement of Serena's marriage obvi-
ated the need for a notice about the termination of her
engagement to Garth.

Those who sought to offer him their sympathy at her
having jilted him for Lord Leland were met with the
fervent response that he counted himself the most fortunate of men to have escaped being leg-shackled to
her.

This prompted elderly dowagers of the *ton* to shake
their heads over the foolish romanticism of the younger
generation that placed the notion of love over obedience
to their parents' wishes. Garth's contemporaries, on the

other hand, cited this case as another prime example of the folly of arranged marriages.

A legion of nubile young ladies of quality proved most eager to help a man as rich and charming as Garth forget Serena. There was much consternation in these ranks when it became clear that Lady Mary Mortley, a diamond of the first water, had distanced the pack of females anxious to become Sir Garth's wife. Speculation was rife among the *ton* that if he had not already thrown the handkerchief to Lady Mary, he was about to do so.

Sally had heard this gossip, and it had wounded her deeply. How quickly Garth had given his love to another. Although he might have forgotten Sally, she would never forget him. She would never again love any other man as she loved him, and she would dedicate herself to becoming one of the great actresses of the London stage.

Despite her determination to concentrate on her acting, Sally desperately longed to see Garth. She knew, however, that he would refuse all overtures on her part and she made none. It was exceedingly painful to know that he was so near her in London and yet so far beyond her reach that he might as well have been on another continent.

Only once had she caught even a glimpse of him in London. He had been riding down Piccadilly in his curricle with an exquisite beauty whom she was certain must have been Lady Mary Mortley. Sally had gone back to her tiny room at the inn where many of the performers at Drury Lane and Covent Garden stayed and had wept the night away.

Sally heard her cue and stepped for the first time onto a London stage. She tried not to notice how enormous the theater was and how many people it held.

No applause greeted her appearance as it had when the well-known actor playing Romeo had strode on stage earlier.

All audiences had to be conquered by a performer,

and the quicker the better. They had to be made to listen and, most important, made to believe that Sally was the character she was portraying.

Unfortunately, her first scene offered her little to say and less opportunity to seize the doubting spectators' attention and earn their respect. The scene—and most of its lines—belonged to the actress playing Juliet's nurse.

Sally's chance would come later in the famous balcony scene, and she would make the most of it. Her future hung in the balance.

As she awaited her cue for the party scene in which Juliet meets Romeo, two late arrivals made their entrance into the tier of boxes adjacent to the stage.

How rude of them, Sally thought, looking up at the haughty beauty in diamonds and silk who looked vaguely familiar. She was followed by a gentleman, elegantly attired in evening dress. An unruly wave of hair fell across his forehead.

Sally's heart began thumping like a wild thing. It was Garth! Belatedly, she recognized his companion as the same woman that she had seen with him in his curricle.

For a moment, Sally felt as though she could not breathe. Oh, God, she could not step on stage and perform before him, especially not when he sat so very close. She had no black Cleopatra's wig to conceal her identity, and he was certain to recognize her.

Garth attentively helped the beauty into her seat. The look that passed between them as he took his own place ripped at Sally's heart and shattered her concentration on the role she was playing.

She missed her cue. It was not an auspicious start to the scene. As she tardily moved on stage for her fateful meeting with Romeo, she tried to concentrate on being Juliet, but in vain. She could think of nothing but Garth.

Her efforts to get back into Juliet's character were further undermined by an audible gasp of recognition from the box where Garth sat so near the stage.

Sally could not stop herself from stealing a glance

up at him. He was leaning forward over the railing of the box, staring down at her.

His face was set in grim, forbidding lines that further unnerved her. Her mind went as blank as a newly scrubbed slate. Romeo spoke to her, but Sally, who had always prided herself on never requiring prompting, could not remember a single word of her lines.

Fortunately, she had not very much to speak, but it still took considerable help for her to get through the scene. She was burningly aware as she left the stage that she had not acquitted herself with distinction.

She would have to do better, much better, in the balcony scene. It would make or break her as an actress upon the London stage.

When Sally appeared on the projection above the stage while Romeo watched from below, she discovered that she was on the same level as Garth's box, and disconcertingly close to it.

As she launched into the famous "O Romeo, Romeo! Wherefore art thou . . ." she could not stop herself from looking toward Garth, her heart crying out her own love to him.

Their eyes met and held for a long moment. She was devastated by the loathing in his gaze.

Then he turned to the lovely woman beside him. Lady Mary gazed adoringly at him. Lifting her bejeweled hand, he slowly, deliberately, bent his head and kissed it.

He might as well have slapped Sally's face.

Anguished memories assaulted her of that day at the cascade when his lips had caressed her hand.

Sally stared with stricken eyes at the tableau in the box. In her abject misery, she forgot not only her lines, but forgot even that she was on the stage of the great Drury Lane Theater making her London debut.

In that instant, what should have been the most thrilling and triumphant night of her young life turned to bitter disaster.

Scattered hisses and boos from the critical audience

at last recalled her to where she was. But her benumbed mind remained a blank. She could not remember her lines.

She could not even recall what role she was playing.

Only the urgent whisperings of the prompter and of the actor playing Romeo got her through the scene. As she exited her balcony at the end of it, she knew the awful shame of having failed as she had never failed before on the stage.

The restive stirrings and murmurings in the audience made it clear that she had lost both its interest and its respect.

Nor was she able to reclaim them. The rest of the night was a long humiliation for her. Garth and his beautiful companion left before the end of the play, as did many others in the audience.

When the terrible ordeal was over, Sally was again hissed and booed during the curtain call.

The disgust she saw on the manager's face told her even before he spoke that her association with Drury Lane had come to an abrupt and untimely end.

Her dream of conquering the London stage had become a nightmare of mortifying failure.

No theater in the city would ever hire her after this disastrous night.

Worse, word of her Drury Lane debacle would quickly travel the theatrical grapevine. Even the better provincial theaters would refuse to hire her now. She would be condemned to spend the rest of her career as a strolling player.

Not only had she lost the only man she had ever loved, but now she had lost the career she had worked so hard to establish.

Whether he meant to or not, Garth had his revenge upon her.

23

Garth, his face a grim mask, strode into the drawing room of his London town house to greet his unexpected caller.

"What a surprise, Lady Wycombe," he said coldly. "I applaud your courage in calling here after the unconscionable fraud you and your husband perpetrated on me. What a hearty laugh you must have had over how easily you were duping me into marrying a common actress."

"No, we did not laugh," Emma protested.

He ignored her denial. "I am glad that you have come, however, for I have a question that has troubled me greatly these past weeks. What did I do to inspire such hatred in you and Thorley that you would strive to humiliate me by tricking me into such a shameful misalliance?"

The color washed from Emma's face. "We wanted you to cry off, not to marry her. I swear we never intended to make a fool of you!"

"What a pity you didn't intend to, for your succeeded magnificently!"

Garth's anger faded a little as he noticed the unmistakable signs of Emma's distress: the trembling hands clutching her reticule, the frightened eyes rimmed with dark circles that bespoke sleepless nights. Clearly she would rather be almost anywhere than here, and he could not help but feel a little sorry for her. Thorley must have forced her to come to beg him to forgive the loans.

Garth had always liked Emma. She had reminded him of her late mother-in-law of whom he had been exceedingly fond. Because of his high estimation of Emma, her participation in the hoax had been particularly hurtful, and he bluntly told her that.

She looked to be on the verge of tears. "Garth, I was persuaded that no two people could be more ill-suited than you and Serena, and I still believe that. You would have been miserable together. I wanted to save you both from that—and save my husband from ruin."

"Then you had only to tell me the truth." His voice was laced with bitterness. "Instead you resorted to that cruel deception."

"I do not blame you for being angry at us. Thorley acted very stupidly, but he was desperate because he could not repay the loans," Emma said sadly. "He was terrified of what would happen to us. You have always been so rich yourself that perhaps you cannot appreciate the panic of a man who faces ruin, especially when he has a wife and child to protect."

Garth regarded Emma through narrowed eyes. "How did Thorley come by the idea for his scheme to deceive me with that actress?"

"You gave it to him."

Garth started to protest, but Emma insisted, "Yes, you did—that night when Thorley brought Sally home and you mistook her for Serena. She tried to tell you the truth then, but you would not listen to her."

A sudden memory flashed into Garth's mind: *I thought she was about to insult my intelligence by attempting to deny that she is Serena.*

"*And you would never believe that, would you?*"

"*Not for a moment, so don't even try.*"

Shaken by this recollection, Garth asked more sharply than he intended, "Have you come to entreat me to forgive the loans or merely for more time to pay them?''

Emma's chin rose proudly. ''Neither. We are doing our best to raise the money.''

Garth knew that was true. They were selling off paintings, furnishings, even Wycombe Abbey and all its land.

''I have come about Sally.''

Emma looked so anxious and unhappy that it flashed through Garth's mind that something must have happened to the sprite. He had told himself that he despised her, that he never wanted to hear her name mentioned again, yet now he found himself demanding urgently, ''What's wrong? Has she met with an accident?''

''No, she—''

He interrupted angrily, ''Did she ask you to come?''

''No, she knows nothing about it. She has fled London.'' Emma's dark eyes were deeply troubled. ''Oh, Garth, how could you have been so cruel to her, deliberately oversetting her like that during her debut at Drury Lane?''

Garth's jaw clenched. He had not meant to do so. Indeed, he cringed at the memory of his behavior that night, but he made no attempt to defend himself to Emma even though his actions had not been premeditated.

He had been late in reaching the theater and had not known that Sally was substituting for the ailing lead actress, had not even known that she was in London. When he had seen her appear on stage, he had been stunned.

Garth had convinced himself that he never wanted to set eyes on her again, yet when he had that night, he had been maddeningly, inexplicably delighted. And that had made him furious at himself as well as her. What had happened after that had been done in a red haze of anger.

''How could you do that to her?'' Emma pressed.

"You dare to ask me that after what she did to me?"

"What she did was love you!"

"What she did was deceive me!" She had hood-winked him into loving her while making a complete fool of him, and he would never be able to forgive her for that.

Emma said quietly, "Had it not been for the decep-tion, you would never have gotten to know each other well enough to fall in love."

"If she came to love me as you contend, she would never have continued to hoax me." He stiffened with anger at Sally Marlowe's perfidy. "The real truth is she set out from the beginning to ensnare me into mar-riage."

"No, the real truth is she followed Thorley's instruc-tions on what to do to get you to cry off. But they did not work, and she fell in love with you. When she re-alized that, she was so desperate that she tried to shock you into ending the engagement that day at the pond."

She had very nearly succeeded. The image flashed through his mind of the sprite after he had pulled her from the water with her soaking chemise plastered to her delectable little body. Even now, to his disgust, that memory still affected his own body in an embarrass-ingly obvious way.

"But after that incident, she became a pattern card of propriety," Garth pointed out. "She did everything she could to please me."

"Yes, she did because by then she was so hopelessly in love with you that she wanted you to see that she could make you a credible wife. And she could, Garth!"

"You call a lying, deceitful actress from the bowels of society a credible wife?"

Emma touched his arm lightly. "Garth, I am con-vinced that you and Sally would be so happy together. What difference does her birth make? Only think how angry you were that Serena thought you were beneath her. Yet you are acting no differently toward Sally."

"It's not the same," he protested.

"Why isn't it?" Emma challenged.

"You know what Sally Marlowe is!"

"Yes, I know what she is: an exciting, spirited beauty of superior understanding who would make you a wife to be proud of if only you would let her!"

"I am the same woman I was yesterday when you were so anxious to marry me . . . It is not I who am different, only your perception of me."

Emma said, "Furthermore, had you married Sally, you would have been no more hoaxed than had you wed Serena."

Garth frowned. "What gammon are you pitching now?"

"Did you never wonder at the amazing likeness between Sally and Serena?"

"More than amazing—incredible," he said bitterly. In his weeks of observing the sprite he had thought so often that no one could change as much as Serena had, that she could not be the same person. Yet, when he had studied her lovely face and delectable body for some physical discrepancy, he could find none at all. That was why his suspicion that she could not be Serena had seemed ridiculous to him. "They could be twins."

"They *are* twins."

For a moment, Garth could only stare in disbelief at Emma. "Explain," he ordered tersely.

Emma told him the story of the Marlowe sisters' birth and separation.

Garth asked in astonishment, "Are you saying that Lady Wycombe never knew the truth?"

"No, she believed until she died that Serena was her own flesh and blood."

The deceit upon the late countess outraged Garth, and he told Emma so.

"Why? She could bear no more children. She most likely would have lost her sanity if she had been told of her baby's death. Instead, she was so happy with Serena. What harm was done?"

Garth could think of no good rejoinder.

"You see, we were all hoaxed," Emma said. "Thorley, Sally, and I had no inkling of the truth until Mrs. Marlowe arrived. Only Serena knew, and she was afraid to tell anyone."

Although Sir Malcolm's motives for wanting to marry his son to Serena had been clear, Garth had not understood—until now—the late earl's surprising willingness to sell his only daughter to the son of a man he neither liked nor respected.

Garth asked scornfully, "Does Lord Leland know yet what he is married to?"

"Yes, he does."

"Will he seek an annulment?"

"No." Emma paused, then continued with an uncharacteristic edge to her voice. "It appears a duke's son with his superior birth can afford to be less concerned about his consequence than a baronet can. Lee loves Serena, and he intends to stand by her."

"He always was a noddy," Garth said contemptuously.

Emma gave him a pitying look. "Oh, Garth, slowtop that Lee is, he is still wise enough to grasp that happiness is more important than pride."

Garth's eyes narrowed angrily. "Lady Mary Mortley will make me both proud and happy."

24

P reston Walcott watched Sally Marlowe, sitting
  alone in a corner of the hall that would serve for
the next two days as his troupe's theater. Since she had
returned to his company from London, she had been
sad and quiet, drained of the vitality and spirit that he
so admired in her. He silently cursed the cruel swell
who was responsible for her misery.

Even her acting was affected, being more mechanical
than inspired now. The debacle of her London debut
had destroyed Sally's confidence in herself. Something
drastic had to be done to restore it, and he intended to
do it.

That was why he informed Sally that she would play
Juliet that night.

What little color she had in her pale face vanished.
She protested in a voiced edged with panic that she
could not possibly do so.

But Preston was adamant. If she were to remain with
his troupe, she must play Juliet.

"It was always your best part," he told her sternly.
"Audiences love you in it."

"Not London audiences!" The humiliation of that
night at Drury Lane was still so potent in her memory
that she cringed at its mere mention. "They all but
booed me off the stage."

"That is why you must play Juliet again—to prove

211

to yourself that what happened that night was an aberration. You must face the specter of defeat and vanquish it.''

''I can't,'' she whispered, knowing that she would be plagued through every moment of the play by the agonizing memory of Garth and Lady Mary Mortley at the Drury.

She swallowed hard. By now, Garth would be betrothed to Lady Mary. When Sally had fled London in disgrace, the announcement had been expected any day. Perhaps they were even married. The thought was like a sword through her heart.

The big, ruddy-faced manager gestured toward the stage, bare of all props.

''I am going to rehearse your scenes with you until you feel confident in the role again. No one else is here so it will be only the two of us.''

Walcott had dismissed the rest of the company, thinking that Sally would be less nervous and intimidated if she knew that no one else would be watching her initially.

He reached out and squeezed her hand reassuringly with his own large paw. ''You are an excellent actress, Sally, and you cannot let one bad night undermine your faith in yourself. I am confident that you will give an outstanding performance tonight. I would not assign you the role if I were not.''

Tears glistened in Sally's eyes at Preston's faith in her. She swore to herself that she would not let him down.

He spent the next ninety minutes rehearsing her in her various scenes. Slowly she began to feel more sure of herself.

Only the balcony scene still gave her trouble. Try as she might, she could not forget that moment when Garth had kissed Lady Mary's hand so lovingly.

Walcott said, ''We will go over that scene one more time, but first, I must talk to a young man who is waiting to see me. I shall be back in a minute or two.''

He strode toward the side door where a handsome stranger had been hovering, watching them rehearse. Undoubtedly, he was an aspiring actor waiting to beg the manager for a place in the company. The troupe had no openings, and Walcott preferred to send him on his way immediately, rather than making him cool his heels.

Besides, until Sally had fully regained her confidence in the balcony scene, Walcott did not want her to realize that she had an audience, even though it was an audience of only one. Fortunately, she had not noticed his presence.

As Sally waited listlessly for Preston Walcott to return, she fingered the letter from Emma in the pocket of her simple muslin gown. The countess wrote her regularly, and this letter had contained a bit of good news. Wycombe Abbey had been sold in its entirety to an anonymous buyer at a better price than the Wycombes had hoped to realize for it. Better yet, the new owner, apparently a rich nabob, had another estate elsewhere that he preferred. Since he would not be using the house, he was agreeable to letting the Wycombes continue to live in it for a while.

Emma made no mention of Garth in her letter, and Sally wondered whether that was because the countess did not want to distress her with word of his marriage to Lady Mary.

With dragging step, Sally positioned herself on the bare stage in the spot where the balcony would be.

As she did, she relived once again in her mind that horrible moment at Drury Lane when Garth had taken Lady Mary's hand. Sally closed her eyes tightly, trying to exorcise that memory, but it was an image that would haunt her until her dying day.

So affected was she by it that it was a moment before she realized that Romeo had begun delivering his lines for the scene:

". . . and Juliet is the sun.

"Arise, fair sun, and kill the envious moon."

Sally froze, convinced that her heartbreak was robbing her of her reason.

Preston Walcott suddenly sounded like Garth.

The rich, caressing voice continued:

"It is my lady, O, it is my love!

"O, that she knew she were!"

Sally's eyes flew open.

Garth stood before her, the wayward wave of golden-brown hair falling across his brow.

For a shocking instant, she feared that she had truly gone mad and was beset by phantom visions.

But then he smiled at her, and she knew that he was real flesh and blood.

Still she could not speak, could not move, could not breathe. Never had she come so close to fainting.

Much as she longed to throw herself into his arms, instinct warned her that more pain would be in store for her if she succumbed to that urge.

Why, after all these agonizing weeks of silence, should he suddenly reappear now? Sally eyed him suspiciously. Had his revenge in London not been enough for him? Was he bent now on seeking some other retribution from her? He had already ruined the Wycombes, costing them even their home.

At last, she managed to croak in a scarcely audible voice, "What are you doing here?"

" 'Begging my love's forgiveness for having been such a fool,' " he said, borrowing again from Shakespeare.

Her heart thumped like a wild bird trying to escape a cage. She started to take a step toward him, then stopped abruptly, remembering with searing clarity his last hateful words to her that awful day in the meadow.

"But you told me you would despise me until your dying day."

He shrugged. It might have been a careless gesture except that his face was suddenly taut and no longer smiling. "Did I? Well, I was wrong as I have been wrong about so many things since you came into my life."

She stared at him uncertainly.

He met her gaze gravely, his eyes as impenetrable as bottomless green pools.

Warily, she asked, "What do you want of me?"

He hesitated, strangely uncertain, as though he were afraid to take the next step.

Finally, he held out his hand to her and said simply, "Come be my love."

Sally started to take his hand before the full import of his words hit her and her heart imploded with pain.

His love, not his wife!

She snatched her hand back as though she had been suddenly stung. Garth wanted to make her his convenient, turn her into the lightskirt he undoubtedly thought all actresses were. He would keep her tucked away until he tired of her, hidden from public view so that his mistress's low origins would not embarrass him.

She could not accept that arrangement. It was an insult to both the permanence and the purity of her love for him. Sally did not want Garth for only a few weeks or months. She cared too much for him to be his fleeting light o' love.

She said coldly, "I thought you did not seek your recreation among the lower orders."

He looked puzzled, then said quietly, his voice husky with emotion, "I am not seeking recreation, my Sprite. I am seeking a wife."

He touched her face with his fingertips, stroking her cheek lightly, lovingly, and a shiver of longing went through her.

Her heart leapt with happiness at the tender entreaty in his eyes until she remembered that there was no hope for them. Just as Romeo and Juliet had been torn apart by feuding families, she and Garth could never close the chasm between social classes that separated them.

"I cannot marry you," Sally said firmly, ignoring the pleading of her heart.

Garth's hand fell away from her cheek. "Are you telling me that you do not love me?"

"No, that I love you too much," she answered honestly. "You will always be ashamed of a wife of my origins, and I could not bear that. Your pride will never permit you to accept me, never permit us to be happy together."

"Ah, yes, 'pride, the never-failing vice of fools,' " Garth quoted sardonically. "I am no longer a fool, my Sprite."

"Perhaps you do not think so." Her voice was sad as a dirge. "But you cannot help despising what I am."

"What you are is precisely what I want for my wife."

Before she realized what he was about, he caught her face in his hands and kissed her slowly, achingly, intensely, his mouth devouring hers.

Pulling back, Sally looked at him with her heart in her eyes. "Are . . . are you certain?"

"After that kiss you can ask me that?" The brilliance of his smile warmed her like a fire on a cold night. "I admit I was slow in recognizing the great disparity between what I thought I wanted in a wife and what made me happy. When I first came home two years ago, I believed that Serena would be the perfect spouse for me, but I was soon bored by her." His green eyes danced with amusement. "With you, Sprite, I shall probably long for occasional boredom."

"What of Lady Mary Mortley?"

He sighed. "Poor Lady Mary, another beautiful example of what I thought I wanted in a wife. But no matter how hard I tried—and God knows I tried very hard—I could not forget you."

"You were so angry at me."

"Yes, I was." His hands stroked her golden curls.

"I used to think myself awake on every suit, and being hoaxed into believing you were Serena made me feel as though I was as stupid as the greenest of Johnny Raws. It took me a long time to comprehend that my rage burned so hot because at its core I was angry at myself. Angry that I could have fallen so deeply in love with a woman of your background that I could not banish you from my memory or my heart."

"My origins have not changed," she pointed out.

"But I understand now that they helped make you the woman I love. Had you grown up in different, more privileged circumstances, you might have been just like your sister—God forbid!"

She looked up at him in surprise. "You know about Serena?"

"Yes, Emma told me."

"Poor Emma and Thorley. You know that Wycombe Abbey no longer belongs to them."

"Yes, it does. I made them a present of it."

Sally's eyes widened in comprehension. "You were the anonymous buyer."

He nodded. "I owed Emma that much. It was she who made me see what a fool I was to think you beneath me."

He opened his arms to Sally, and she stepped into them.

"Oh, my darling," he groaned, hugging her so fiercely to him that she could scarcely breathe. "I was afraid I would never hold you like this again."

No more afraid than Sally had been. She reveled in the strength of his arms around her, feeling comforted, protected, loved.

He nibbled at her ear, sending shivers of excitement through her, then murmured, "You have not told me yet whether you will marry me, fair Juliet. 'Exchange thy love's faithful vow for mine.' "

" 'I give thee mine before thou didst request it.' " Sally tipped her head and smiled at him. "And like Juliet's for Romeo, my love for you is infinite."

"As is mine for you, my Sprite," he assured her, his warm breath teasing her ear. "We shall be married at Wycombe Abbey. Emma insists."